To whomever &

I hope you enjoy it.

THE MISSING PIECE
OF MY SOUL

*The devine gift of love, rescue,
revelation, and the quiet wisdom
that lingers after love ends.*

ZAC BRADMAN

Copyright © 2026 Zac Bradman.

All rights reserved. No part of this book may be used or reproduced by any means, graphic, electronic, or mechanical, including photocopying, recording, taping or by any information storage retrieval system without the written permission of the author except in the case of brief quotations embodied in critical articles and reviews.

This is a work of fiction. All of the characters, names, incidents, organizations, and dialogue in this novel are either the products of the author's imagination or are used fictitiously.

Balboa Press books may be ordered through booksellers or by contacting:

Balboa Press
A Division of Hay House
1151 W. 2nd St
Bloomington IN 47403
www.balboapress.co.uk
UK TFN: 0800 0148647 (Toll Free inside the UK)
UK Local: (02) 0369 56325 (+44 20 3885 6882 from outside the UK)

Because of the dynamic nature of the Internet, any web addresses or links contained in this book may have changed since publication and may no longer be valid. The views expressed in this work are solely those of the author and do not necessarily reflect the views of the publisher, and the publisher hereby disclaims any responsibility for them.

The author of this book does not dispense medical advice or prescribe the use of any technique as a form of treatment for physical, emotional, or medical problems without the advice of a physician, either directly or indirectly. The intent of the author is only to offer information of a general nature to help you in your quest for emotional and spiritual well-being. In the event you use any of the information in this book for yourself, which is your constitutional right, the author and the publisher assume no responsibility for your actions.

Any people depicted in stock imagery provided by Getty Images are models, and such images are being used for illustrative purposes only. Certain stock imagery © Getty Images.

Print information available on the last page.

ISBN: 979-8-7652-1667-5 (sc)
ISBN: 979-8-7652-1666-8 (e)

Library of Congress Control Number: 2026903840

Balboa Press rev. date: 02/10/2026

CHAPTER 1

THERE WAS NO GETTING AWAY FROM IT.

No matter how many times I chastised myself for being weak and always going back.

Or how much I tried to reason with myself that it was the wrong thing to do and that it was a toxic relationship I was chasing.

Nor how many times my friends told me to walk away, turn the page and move on.

And it didn't matter how often I was ghosted or how many times I was blocked and unblocked.

I was caught and couldn't get away.

Because this was the love of my life…the missing piece of my soul …and I knew it…

…before I even knew his name.

CHAPTER 2

IT WAS ANOTHER GLORIOUS MORNING IN MY ISLAND RETREAT AS I AWOKE to the tranquil sounds of the crystal clear, turquoise waters lapping the shore and the sea breeze gently rustling the palm trees of my beach front villa. Who needs an alarm? I asked myself. For the past 5 years, I have woken up this way, and I have never tired of it. Even though the property was expensive to buy at the time, it was worth every penny to have this little bit of paradise, tucked away at the end of a beautiful, private beach with white sand and palm trees. It was the epitome of the idyllic tropical island hideaway that we have all probably dreamt of at some stage in our lives.

As I sat up in the huge, super king-sized bed, pillows and cushions scattered all over the place as testament to another fitful night's sleep, and trying to orient myself to a new day, I looked around the spacious room with its high vaulted ceiling, chaise longue off to the left, and floor to ceiling glass patio doors on three sides. Ok, maybe it sounds like I lived in a fishbowl but the early morning sun, shining through the thin, peach colored voile curtains added a warm glow to the otherwise beige and neutrally colored decor. I couldn't help but think to myself how thankful I was to be able to live like this.

I drank in the serene splendor for a moment as I looked out across the private living room of the master suite, then the Koi Pond and garden, to the ocean beyond. After a couple of minutes of letting my eyes adjust to the light of the day, I straightened the pillows, slid across to the edge of the bed and sank my weary old feet into the plush, shag pile rug that extended out from under the bed in all directions.

As always, I was once again reminded of the harsh reality that I was waking up alone. Letting out a wistful sigh, I pondered how close

I came to achieving that utopia we all seek, what we often refer to as heaven on earth. Every material aspect of this paradise that I had carved out for myself, whether by hard work or sheer good fortune, had all fallen into place to make it a reality and, despite not having anyone to share it with, I was eternally grateful for everything I had.

Spread over two floors, the front of the property was a single level which faced the beach and the ocean with a beautiful infinity pool and various outdoor living areas designed to make the most of the sea views. All the public reception rooms were on this level, including lounges and dining spaces, a kitchen with an open-plan breakfast area, a full bar and huge media room.

The clever architectural design saw many rooms spanning the full width of the building with at least 2 walls made of floor to ceiling glass patio doors, curtains and drapes, just like those of the master suite. This feature allowed an incredible amount of light and fresh air to pass through every room, which created an amazing indoor-outdoor living feel throughout the entire property.

Most of the outdoor dining and living areas were covered with extensions of the main roof with the same vaulted ceilings supported by white brick pillars that were a recurring theme throughout. They also blended, seamlessly, with the covered walkways that connected the various areas of the property.

Due to the gentle slopping nature of the land, the rear of the property was on two levels, built in a 'U' shape that enclosed the secluded garden which was bound by plant beds and box hedging. There were copious palm trees of various sizes, some of which reached up as far as the second level and beyond. They kept the rear of the property cool and added a distinctly tropical feel to the whole place, with a serene rustling of leaves whenever there was a nice sea breeze.

Sure, the house was probably far too big for one person to live in, and expensive to run, but I didn't care. I was truly thankful that I could finally easily afford it, but above all, I loved being there. It felt almost perfect for me, and I never wanted to leave.

Alas, there was one missing piece that was always just out of reach and beyond my control. How desperately I wanted to share all of this with him, to be able to wake up the way I do…but cuddled in his gorgeous arms. That feeling of warmth and security, safe in the belief that no matter what went on in the world while we slept, nothing could ever hurt me, so long as I was with him.

Sadly, it wasn't to be. So, every morning, without fail, I'd sit alone on the edge of my bed, I'd think of him and wonder if he was ok and hoped he was happy, wherever he was.

Feeling the pang in my heart from the wound that had never healed, and that all too familiar lump that developed in my throat, I let out another sigh as I got up and headed to the ensuite bathroom to complete, my all too familiar, morning ritual.

CHAPTER 3

LIKE TRYING TO PUSH START A BEATEN-UP OLD CAR, I STARTED WITH A little morning meditation and yoga to get things moving. Then a luxurious shower followed by a shave and a trim of my grey goatee. All the while staring at something in the mirror that looked like a cross between Gollam and Yoda and wondering to myself, what the hell is that?! After dressing, I would head out to the main kitchen where I hoped, as always, Mara was there ready to prepare some breakfast for me.

Mara and her husband Paulo managed the place, and they basically looked after me. They were the sweetest Portuguese couple that I kind of inherited when I bought the property and, not only did they remain faithful staff members all that time, but over the years they became very good friends, almost family, and I really didn't know what I would have done without them. They lived on-site in their own 2-bedroom apartment, which was annexed to the main part of the house, and they were my absolute go to people for just about everything you can imagine.

Paulo took care of the property in terms of its structure. He maintained the gardens, which were always immaculate, cleaned the pool and oversaw any specialist trades people we might, from time to time, have needed. Paulo was also a keen fisherman, a great golf buddy, willing taxi driver come chauffer and an excellent skipper. After so many years, he knew the canals and backwaters of the island like the back of his hand, so he was always at the helm whenever we took the boat out.

Mara took care of the food. The kitchen was her domain and heaven help anyone who messed it up! She was an amazing cook, and I often thought she had missed her calling as a chef. She kept me so well fed I had to do a workout every day in the gym downstairs, just to avoid becoming the size of the house in which we all resided. Mara also oversaw the domestic help that we had coming in on a regular basis to take care of the laundry and cleaning of this extensive property. She had a keen eye and as a result, like the gardens, the house was always immaculately presented and spotlessly clean.

The property had an additional 5 ensuite bedrooms on the lower level, which were rented out from time to time, either as individual Airbnb rooms or collectively for various types of retreats. All of which helped to contribute to the running costs of the property. Paulo and Mara were amazing hosts, from doing meet-and-greet at the airport to organizing private excursions to the surrounding islands for guests. Being very sociable, they seemed to really enjoy the comings and goings of lots of different people, plus their knowledge of the island, and how things worked there, were invaluable in keeping the whole place running like a well-oiled machine.

"Good morning!" Mara greeted me with her usual radiant smile. "Did you sleep ok?"

"Like a babe!" I said, "I must have had some bizarre dreams though because I woke up in a tangled mess with pillows all over the place, plus I am starving! What's for breakfast?"

"Your usual 'Greena-Colada' smoothie and I have a fresh batch of croissants, or would you prefer a cooked breakfast if you are so hungry."

She named it 'Greena-Colada' one day as a joke because it was primarily made with fresh banana and pineapple, but also had a generous handful of spinach, which turned it green. Now, none of us could ever imagine it being called by any other name.

"No, just the smoothie, a couple of croissants and coffee would be perfect. I want to do a workout this morning before Jason arrives, so I better take it easy."

Just then, Paulo walked into the kitchen and joined me as I sat at the breakfast bar. "How ya doing?" he asked in his normal casual style as Mara handed him a coffee and a croissant.

"Oh, you know…still alive!"

"Isn't Jason arriving today? Shall I collect him from the airport?"

"Thanks, that's kind of you to offer, but I think I will go and collect him. It's been such a long time since he was last here and I'm dying to see him"

"Ok. Let me know if you change your mind."

Never one to be able to sit still for more than 5 minutes, Paulo got up from the breakfast bar. "Well, some of us have things to do," he quipped. He grabbed his croissant and coffee, gave Mara a quick peck on the cheek, and left to continue his morning routine, leaving me to finish my breakfast in silence.

"You seem awfully pensive this morning" said Mara, "got something on your mind?"

"Nothing specific" I said as I got up from the breakfast bar and took my empty dishes to the dishwasher. "Just the usual, same old same old."

"I do wish you would meet someone else to take your mind off him. It's not good to dwell on things that might have been."

"Yeah, yeah. You know I've tried that many times, but nothing ever seems to work. Anyway, thank you for caring, but right now, I too have things to do." I lightly kissed Mara on the cheek. "I'll see you later," and with that, I took my coffee, headed out of the kitchen and walked along the upstairs walkway, towards my office at the far end of the building. All the while I ran my fingers through the palm leaves that flowed over the railing like a suspended green wave that sparkled in the morning sunlight.

CHAPTER 4

I settled at my desk and looked around the office as I fired up my PC. I loved my office. It was my sacred workspace, and I spent quite a lot of my time there. I had a large desk with a beveled front edge, which was wonderful for putting my feet up, because the edge of the desk didn't cut into the back of my legs cutting off the circulation. Ok, perhaps it was not the prescribed way to sit at a computer, sit up straight, feet flat on the floor, thighs parallel with the floor and all that. Of course, Mara chastised me frequently about how I sat, but it was super comfortable, and somehow, I just seemed to think better that way.

As was common throughout the property, the marble tiled floor was covered almost entirely with a large rug that extended out from under the desk in all directions. Opposite the desk was a small sofa on which I sometimes stretched out to read during the day. The sofa sat in front of the customary floor to ceiling glass patio doors allowing plenty of natural light to enter the space. Looking out, all I could see was a sea of green palm leaves stretching up from the garden below which reflected the dappled sunlight, filling my office with a soft green hue and a definite sense of relaxation that came from sitting in nature.

Off to the left, the wall was partly lined with shelves containing a myriad of books from fiction to self-help; poetry books by my favorite poet Percy Bysse Shelley; my indispensable collection of books by Dr Wayne W. Dyer; books on business; and investing for dummies! The rest of the wall space was taken up by my 1.5 meter by 1 meter print of Café Terrace de Nuit by Van Gogh, which I absolutely loved getting lost in. No matter how often or how long I stared at it, something new always seemed to creep out at me.

After a moment of gratitude for my wonderful surroundings, I began my usual browsing of the internet, starting with the BBC News website. Never having been one for politics, football or in-depth current events, I skimmed the headlines for anything remotely interesting, but more just to make sure the world wasn't nuked by one fanatical leader or another while I slept. Satisfied that, overall, we lived to spin another day on the world's axis, I popped over to Facebook.

Again, never being one for social media and firmly of the belief that it was the scourge of the modern world, which was probably what my great grandparents said about television, I aimlessly scrolled through the posts while I drank my coffee. I couldn't, for the life of me, understand why I wasted my time with such dribble. Being an intensely private person, I can't remember the last time I posted anything. Mostly, I would simply use it to check up on friends and family, but not having any contact with them on a regular basis kind of made it seem like a pointless ritual. However, like many habits, there was some comfort to be had from this daily, mindless activity.

Eventually, having finished my coffee, I dragged myself away and got into doing some real work. First there was the budget and spending to update. Scanning through all my various bank accounts and investment portfolios for the latest transactions, I documented everything into a spreadsheet. I know it may sound petty, and even anal to some, but it was my grandmother who always used to say, "Look after the pennies and the pounds will look after themselves" and how right she was.

Gone are the days when I used to live from paycheck to paycheck wondering how I would manage to buy groceries during that last week of the month. That week when I would invariably be vowing to do better next month as I scoured the depths of my cupboard, hoping to be able to cobble together something remotely edible from dried spaghetti, a few stock cubes and half a bottle of Heinz tomato ketchup. Of course, like a hamster on a wheel, that same stressful pattern would go on month after month, year in and year out.

Like most of us, I had to learn things the hard way and eventually, when I was struggling to pay rent in Paris and a mortgage in Porto, I was forced to keep track of every cent I was spending and choose carefully what to spend it on. That was the start of my daily habit, which continues to this very day, and it has made a huge difference to my finances over the years.

Despite being what you might call semi-retired for the past 10 years, I always seemed to have a ton of work to do. It didn't really feel like work because I didn't have a boss or anyone to report to, so I did the things I chose when I chose to do them. I didn't really need the money either, so I guess it was more like a hobby. However, it did give me a sense of purpose, a feeling of belonging and maybe even being needed, plus it helped to stop my brain from turning into a pile of mush! So, I guess that was a good thing.

However, today was not really going to be a workday. Having done my daily stint of cooking the books, the rest of the day was going to be a day of leisure, starting with a workout. So, I shut down my PC and headed downstairs to the gym.

The gym was massive by your average home gym standards. I thought it was amazing and one of the many features of the property that I loved when I bought it.

It was fully equipped and I mean fully equipped. It probably had more equipment than many public gyms. There were cardio machines including bikes, cross trainers, a stair master and rowing machines. There were resistance machines for all parts of the body including a kinetic installation that kept my golf swing in top form. My golf was still rubbish though, as Paulo constantly delighted in reminding me!

Of course there was a free weights area, no gym would be complete without one, and even a punch bag hanging from the ceiling, should I ever have felt the need to beat the crap out of something.

Best of all, however, there was a sauna and a steam room which I absolutely loved.

So, first things first, I went over and fired up the sauna and steam room, which allowed them to come up to temperature while I did my workout. Then it was onto one of the cardio machines for a 10-minute warmup, followed by whatever body part workout was scheduled for the day. Normally I would do my workout in the afternoon but, as Jason was arriving soon, I decided it would be best to get it out of the way in the morning.

Once done with exercising, I spent half an hour or so switching between the sauna, steam room and the shower. Did all that effort make any difference? Probably not visibly. At my age I was never going to be Arnold Schwarzenegger, but at least it kept my 'dad bod' in reasonable condition and maybe staved off the inevitable decline that comes with advancing years.

By now it was getting close to lunchtime, so after a quick snack, I had just enough time for my daily stroll along the beach.

The beach was completely private and each property along the beach owned a stretch of it, which was equivalent to the width of their respective property boundaries, all the way down to the water's edge.

It was not a long beach, being only about 1000 meters to the beach club, which sat toward the far end, but it was long enough to keep the circulation going. I also found it extremely therapeutic to be able to walk along in the shallow, crystal-clear tropical water, as the waves gently lapped up against my ankles. Any stresses or problems I may have been struggling with from time to time seemed to get washed away by the tide.

CHAPTER 5

Back at the house after my daily constitutional, I washed the sand from my feet in the outdoor shower by the pool, threw on my shoes and jumped in the car. I lived very close to the airport, and as I was pulling out of the driveway, I saw Jason's flight coming in for landing. It was only a 5-minute drive to the main terminal, so I still had plenty of time.

Finding a convenient spot in the short-term parking area, I made my way across the parking lot, past the ever-present line of taxis waiting eagerly to whisk away any new arrivals who, no doubt, were probably desperate to get to their accommodation so they could get out in the sun as soon as possible.

Even though we were just an island, being a very popular destination meant the airport was serviced by many international flights from other Caribbean Islands, the USA, Canada and places further afield like Europe. With the constant increase in tourism, the airport had evolved into a reasonable size with all the standard amenities you'd find at larger destinations.

Entering the arrivals hall, I looked around and saw the familiar collection of private drivers and tour operators all waiting with their placards announcing the names of the passengers they had been sent to collect. The arrivals hall was spacious with very high ceilings designed to keep things as cool as possible, as it could get pretty warm on the island, particularly during the summer.

Along the wall, opposite where the passengers exited after passing through immigration, the baggage hall and customs, there was a Relay newsagent, and a souvenir store selling locally made items and gazillions of fridge magnets and bottle openers that you really didn't know you couldn't live without. There was also a Starbucks coffee shop where some of the meet and greeters could be seen chatting with each other over a coffee as they waited patiently for their respective arrivals.

It was a small island and basically everyone knew each other, and I nodded silent greetings to many of the locals as I moved off to one side so Jason could spot me more easily, not that I didn't stand out with my very white hair. As I stood there looking around, I couldn't help but get the feeling that I could be at almost any airport in the world. I let out a bit of a sigh as I noted how unimaginative and almost sterile much of the world had become.

It didn't take long before the first passengers started to emerge, some a little weary after a long flight from Paris and some clearly a little overwhelmed, as they scanned the waiting crowd, anxiously hoping their pre-arranged collector had actually turned up.

Suddenly, he emerged carrying nothing more than a backpack and I noticed that he hadn't changed a bit since I last saw him. Jason was my younger half-sister's son and my favorite nephew. Ok, he was my only nephew, but still my favorite. Some years after my parents split, my father remarried and started a new family, which my sister was part of, hence my much younger nephew, Jason.

Now in his late 20's Jason had been living in Paris for a while. Being a 6 foot 2, well-toned, reasonably handsome and masculine young man, it was a bit of a surprise, especially to his mother, when he came out as gay. Having recently broken up with his latest boyfriend, he called me asking if he could come and stay. He said he just needed to get away for a bit, but I couldn't help but notice something in his voice that told me he also wanted to talk with his favorite, Uncle Charlie.

He suddenly saw me off to the side and approached with a huge smile on his face, "Welcome Jason, it's good to see you my boy," I said with genuine affection. He really was special, and it was always wonderful when he was able to spend some time with me. "I am really glad you made it."

"You're looking really well too, uncle," commented Jason as he stooped a little and gave me a big bear hug and a kiss on each cheek, in typical Parisian fashion.

"Well, it's a hard life of sun, sand and sea breeze, but someone's gotta do it," I chuckled.

Confident that he had everything, namely his backpack, we headed for the car. Even though I hadn't been in the terminal for very long, the car was already unbearably hot inside. Throwing the windows down, we set off with the wind blasting only slightly cooler air as we drove along. "How was your flight?"

"It was fine, uneventful as always. Air France is a nice airline to fly with and having a direct service here makes it so much easier," said Jason nonchalantly, but I could tell he was kind of distracted, and he clearly had more on his mind.

With both of us probably thinking it was best to wait until we got home before getting into any serious discussion, we indulged in inane, idle chit chat about the weather and my health, and anything else we could come up with, to avoid any of the issues that I suspected may have been burning away in the background.

After a few minutes, we pulled into the cool garage of the house. I showed Jason to his room where he unceremoniously dumped his backpack on the bed. Clearly, he was a lot more tired from the flight than he was letting on. So, I left him to sort himself out, freshen up, shower or whatever, and headed upstairs.

CHAPTER 6

Passing by the kitchen, I grabbed some cold juice from the refrigerator and headed to the outdoor lounge area. It really was quite a hot day for this time of the year, but fortunately there was a lovely, gentle sea breeze which took the edge off.

I loved the outdoor lounge. It had a beige colored sofa arranged in a 'U' shape around a large, glass-topped coffee table which was ideal as a conversation area with friends, or just to sit, relax and watch the ocean as I sometimes did.

Settling in amongst the cushions, I flicked to the page where I left off in the book I was reading called 'Fundamentals – Ten Keys to Reality' by Frank Wilczek.

When I lived in Porto, I found it quite difficult to find English books, not that I was a great reader in those days, but occasionally I would take a book with me to the beach and pretend to read it whilst discreetly ogling the sights of the nearly naked men sunbathing in the dunes all around me.

Once a year there was the annual book fair and FNAC would always have an English book section. As I was starting to develop my spiritual side of things with meditation, I was drawn to the 'Ten Keys to Reality' in the title. However, as it was only one, in a pile of books I had bought that day, it ended up spending most of its life sitting on the shelf gathering dust…until now.

"What ya reading?" enquired Jason as he stepped out onto the terrace and came over to join me on the sofa.

I didn't reply, I just held the book up so he could read the title.

"Yikes" he said.

"Yeah, it isn't quite the reality I thought it was going to be from the title. It's all about Atoms and Protons, Quarks and Gluons, the building blocks of the world around us and the Universe at large!"

"Hmmm, entertaining?" asked Jason.

"Probably not the adjective I would choose"

"Interesting?"

"I guess"

"Informative!?"

"Yeah, probably would be if I could understand it!"

Marking my page, I threw the book onto the sofa next to my feet, just as Mara emerged from the kitchen with a batch of her famous, freshly baked scones, complete with jam and whipped cream. So much for all the calories I struggled to burn off this morning.

"The kettle's on and I thought you boys might be hungry."

"Oh, yum!" exclaimed Jason as his eyes almost popped out of his head suggesting he was rather hungry after his long flight.

Mara quickly scurried away and returned a few moments later with a tea tray and some homemade lemonade. Being highly intuitive, she looked at us both and said "Well, I'll leave you two to chat," and with that she turned away, leaving behind the perfect segway for me to get into some more serious discussion with Jason.

"So how have you been since breaking up with your boyfriend?"

"Yeah, ok I guess"

"Do you want to tell me about it?"

There was a bit of a pause as he sat there with a glum look on his face.

"It was just the same as all the others. It started out fine and then after a couple of months, it all went kind of weird."

"How so?" I asked.

"For the first few weeks, we always met out or were at my place. He seemed nice, and I liked him. He was big into photography and sometimes we would go out early in the morning to catch the sunrise. Meeting at 6:00am was a challenge because I don't do mornings, but I thought, maybe, he might be worth the effort."

"Fair enough."

"Then one day we went back to his place after doing a photo shoot and spent the afternoon sunbathing on his terrace. That's when I started to find out more about him."

"Like what?"

"Well, it turned out he was a bit of a crossdresser and was super excited about the hot pink stilettos he had recently purchased."

Knowing that Jason, like me, prefers his men to be men with a large dollop of masculinity, I couldn't help but snigger as I bit my lip to suppress a full-on giggle. "Didn't you have any inclination of this beforehand?"

"No, not at all. I thought he was very masculine, with a full beard, super hairy chest and not the least bit effeminate in any way. In fact, he was even a bit dominant."

"So did he model them for you?" I sniggered again.

"Oh yeah! Bearing in mind that he was only 5 foot 4, stocky and we were sunbathing on his terrace, the look of pink stilettos, short hairy legs and blue speedos, didn't really do it for me,"

"Oh dear!" I said as I tried my best to stifle another laugh.

"To be honest the fact that he likes stilettos didn't really bother me. I mean, each to their own, right? However, he then started proudly showing me the photos of him out with his friends in full drag and makeup, still with the beard, plunging neckline, which was clearly designed to show off his hairy chest, along with the pink stilettos at the end of his short hairy legs. Well, that was when the romance went right out the window for me," laughed Jason.

Unable to control myself, I burst out laughing as my mind concocted the image that Jason had just described.

"Well, that was one thing, which wasn't really the problem, but then I found he had some more concerning issues," continued Jason as we both tried to regain our composure.

"I'm not sure I want to ask but go on."

"Well, he had his own weed farm in his closet. He said he needed to have a continuous supply, because he says smoking it just before sex was the only way he could get hard."

"Oh yeah, I've met guys like that before. Really does wonders for your ego, knowing they need something else to get turned on."

"But that wasn't all, I then discovered he was having to take some sort of prescription sleeping tablets, or anti-depressants or something, at night to be able to sleep. Then he had to set the alarm for 5:00am so he could then take something else that would help him wake up in the morning. It needed time to kick in to his system, and if he missed taking it, he wouldn't be able to get out of bed in time for work."

"Oh, that really doesn't sound good."

"Yeah, sadly, I really couldn't see this working out between us, so I had to end it."

CHAPTER 7

As I sat there listening to Jason's story my mind immediately flashed back to my own terrible experience of someone who indulged in what is sometimes known as Chem Sex.

"Well, it's a good thing you knocked it on the head straight away before you developed any deep feelings for him. Once that happens, you can find yourself making all sorts of excuses for their behavior and can easily get sucked into that world before you know it," I said knowingly.

"Really? Sounds like you got involved with someone who was into that sort of stuff?"

"Yeah, I knew a guy who liked to smoke a pipe. But it wasn't just any old tobacco pipe, this was a glass pipe. He would drop a white, fine-grained substance into it, then heat it with a blow torch and inhale the resulting smoke. As I understood it, the idea being that he would feel more alert, stay awake for longer and feel less inhibited during sex."

"Oh!? You mean Crystal-Meth?" asked Jason with a look of shock all over his face.

"Yeah, maybe. I was never 100% sure what it was but I suspected it was that, though he vehemently denied that it was any kind of drug. Anyway, the effects on his personality were distinctly noticeable when he was smoking it. In fact, there was sufficient difference from the original guy that I coined a new persona for him and dubbed him 'The Pipe Man'. It wasn't extreme changes, I mean we are not talking Dr Jekyll and Mr. Hyde here, but the differences in him were there just the same."

"I assume you immediately ran away from him?"

"No. I should have, and all my friends told me to, but I had fallen very much in love with the original, sober guy."

"Really? So, what happened?"

"Not long into the 'relationship' if you can call it that, I agreed to hop on a flight and go stay with him for a long weekend, which was wonderful. He was kind and generous, wouldn't let me pay for anything all weekend. He was thoughtful, attentive, tender and sensual. He cooked for me and wouldn't let me help or do the dishes or anything. He was the most gracious host and really treated me like a King."

"Sounds great!"

"Yeah, however, as the weekend progressed, I came to the realization that 'The Pipe Man' had had a rather heavy, all night pipe session the night before I arrived. As a result, the original sober guy was suffering the effects of coming off the high, all weekend, which got progressively worse, with lethargy playing a big part. That is until he obviously couldn't stand it any longer and went out on the Monday, got a 'fix' and 'The Pipe Man' returned."

"So, what happened?"

"It was obvious that he was out with friends with little intention of spending any of the last day with me. So, after a confused discussion on the phone, he returned home to take me to the airport early. Clearly, he was in a very animated and agitated state and was kind of hyper, not to mention just a little pissed off that my presence was interrupting his afternoon of 'fun'. I could smell the smoke on him the instant he walked in. My natural response was to ask him if he had been smoking, which he denied and then called me crazy."

"What did you do?"

"Well, I wasn't his husband or boyfriend and therefore probably had no right to question him, so I let it slide, and I let him take me to the airport. However, on the way, still clearly annoyed that I had messed up his afternoon after he had so generously spent 2 days with me, and obviously considered that my visit was over, he tried to tell me that my problem was I craved attention."

"What?! Are you serious?!"

"Yep, and as you know, I most definitely do not. I prefer to stay in the shadows or the corner of the room at any social gathering as opposed to being the center of attention."

"Hmm…That sounds very narcissistic to me."

"Yep, he tried to make me the villain and him the innocent victim. It almost worked too, until I realized later that it is in fact he who craves attention by having multiple sexual partners throughout the course of a single day, and he was simply projecting his character traits onto me."

"Well, at least you got away from him, right?"

"Ummm…No, not exactly."

"You kept seeing him?!"

"Yeah, as I said, I was completely in love with the original, sober guy and so I continued to see him over the course of about 9 months, though I saw him somewhat infrequently due to his job. Because I was in love with him, I kept hoping that each time, things would be different. Maybe he might have gotten this 'phase' out of his system, and we could have a 'normal' loving relationship. Unfortunately, love, reason and hope are no match for drugs and simply crumble in the face of an addiction."

"So, I take it things didn't improve?"

"No. They got progressively worse as his addiction took more of a hold on him. I paid close attention to things that happened, and concluded, that 'The Pipe Man' didn't really like me, but he tolerated me as I was a convenience. I made finding additional partners for group sex easier for him, especially at 8:00am on a Monday morning. However, that didn't stop him from treating me badly and sometimes doing things that hurt me…emotionally not physically."

"I assume you eventually stopped seeing him?"

"Well, everything came to a head, one day when I was with him. I met him first thing in the morning at his hotel as usual. Once we settled into his room, I was delighted when he announced that 'today it would be just us, just the two of us, I promise', he said. I was overjoyed at this. Finally, the guy I loved with all my heart and soul was going to be spending an entire day alone with me. However, in no time at all, out came the pipe and 'The Pipe Man' soon appeared and took over. Within a very short time, he was on his phone, surfing the internet for guys and paying absolutely no attention to me, whatsoever. After a couple of hours, the first guy turned up at the room for a threesome. So much for the promise of us being alone."

"Oh! What did you do?"

"I made excuses for him in my head and after a while, the guy left. I tried to draw a veil over it by trying to just enjoy the moment of being alone with the man I loved so much once again. However, before long, a second guy turned up and the same scenario ensued. Afterwards, the second guy and 'The Pipe Man' began speaking quietly together in French as if they were plotting something. My spoken French was desperately lacking in confidence, but my understanding of French wasn't as bad. I noted what was being said from the few words that I could hear, tucked it away in the back of my brain but didn't really dwell on it too much. The guy gave 'The Pipe Man' his number and left. When I quizzed 'The Pipe Man', he said that the guy wasn't his type and that he was just being diplomatic, so I thought nothing more of it."

"And then what?"

"You guessed it. A third guy turned up as clearly 'The Pipe Man' was on a roll. This guy was horrible! He had dreadful energy, and I didn't like him at all. The same scenario played out until I couldn't take it anymore and stormed off to the bathroom to regain my composure. However, I am sure 'The Pipe Man' thought I was just being a wuss and non-compliant."

"He clearly didn't give a shit about you."

"Nope and, as I returned to the room, 'The Pipe Man' leapt to his feet, alarmed at a sudden meeting he had to attend, threw on some clothes and left in a hurry. On his way out he suggested the other guy stay with me. However, as he was clearly not interested in me, he took to his scrappers and left, which I was very relieved about, leaving me abandoned and alone in the room."

"So, what did you do?"

"I naturally waited for him to return. I waited and waited, and time slowly marched on as 1, 2, 3 hours passed, and I was still alone with no sign of either 'The Pipe Man', nor my original, sober guy whom I loved so much. I started to contemplate going home and began organizing my bags but didn't want to simply leave without saying anything. As I looked around the room, I noticed that the meth pipe and little bag of 'stuff' were nowhere to be found. I pondered this for some time wondering why he would have taken these items to the meeting. Wouldn't that be a bit risky if his colleagues found out? I checked the time he left, which was about 5:30pm and then the cogs started whirring and things started to fall into place."

"What?"

"That conversation with the second guy, that I had stored away in the back of my brain, suddenly came to the forefront of my mind. I went through what I had gleaned from the conversation, that was happening right in front of me, and then it dawned on me. They were planning a rendezvous at 6:00pm. No wonder he was gone for so long. 'The Pipe Man' clearly decided that he wanted to hook-up with others, without me being present, and, thinking I was stupid, conducted the entire conversation in French because he thought I wouldn't understand what they were saying and wouldn't work out what was going on."

"You've gotta be kidding?"

"No, and I was deeply hurt that he had the audacity to do this right in front of me. No wonder he took the meth pipe et al to the meeting. He intended to go directly from there to the hook-up, without having to return to the room as he would have had to have concocted some story as to where he was going again and why. That is assuming there was actually a meeting at all."

"So, then what did you do?"

"I sent a message asking if I should go home, to which I received no response for the next hour. He eventually came back with some crap story about a colleague and having to take her to the hospital but would be back soon. However, that too was nothing but more lies and manipulation, and eventually he told me to go home."

"Wow! Please don't tell me you saw him again after all that!"

"It was a very sad day for me as I decided that I never wanted to see 'The Pipe Man' again. Obviously, even though I felt they were different personas, they were still ultimately the same guy, whom I loved with all my heart, but knew the chances of ever seeing him again without 'The Pipe Man' were slim at best. Completely heartbroken, I began to remove all traces of him from my life and tried my best to move on."

"I can't believe you put yourself through all of that and didn't just walk away at the beginning when you saw all the red flags."

"I know...I should have, you're right, and so was everyone else. However, there was something about him that stopped me walking away. Something I felt deep inside that I chose to listen to rather than face facts, and once you have that deep feeling for someone, it can be very hard to extricate yourself. Love makes you blind and you end up doing things that rationally, you would never consider doing. You make excuses for their behavior, you draw a veil over things, and you keep hoping that things will change, but they rarely do, especially when addiction is involved. All you do is teach them that it is ok for them to treat you the way they do. Before you know it, you've been sucked into their world, and once you are there, everything can very easily spiral out of control."

"Wow! I never knew you had gone through something like that."

"Well, it was a long time ago, but that's why I think you getting out early from your last relationship was probably for the best and I think you may have dodged a bullet there. Just chalk it up to experience, try to avoid guys who are into stuff like that, and see if you can move on."

"Yeah, I am trying to, but he is just the latest in what is becoming a bit of a long line of disasters and false starts. It's a struggle being gay, especially in Paris where most people only seem to be interested in anonymous hookups and nothing more. I find life in Paris can be kind of lonely at times and it really gets me down. Sometimes I am not even sure if it is the right lifestyle for me, being gay and all."

"Really? What makes you say that?" I asked Jason, somewhat surprised. As far as I knew, Jason had never had a girlfriend, and I was pretty sure he was always gay.

"Sometimes I look at my straight friends and think their lives are less complicated. Everything seems to fit better for them, and they don't seem to experience things like weird behaviors, drugs and even fetishes to the same extent."

"Ha! Jason, you're just in a slump right now and at times like this, the grass always looks particularly greener on the other side. It's not the choice of lifestyle that is the issue; it is the people we come across and let into our lives that makes things complicated and messy. Believe me, it is a crazy world out there and you'll find people with the same issues in all walks of life if you look hard enough."

"Hmmm, I guess," mused Jason.

"You don't sound convinced, so tell me…why do you choose to date men?"

Jason sat for a minute and stared into space. Shrugging his shoulders he said "I don't know. I guess I was always more comfortable hanging out with guys than girls. I went to an all-boys school, so was always hanging out with them, rather than girls, as I was growing up."

"Did you ever try dating girls when you were younger?" I asked.

"Not really. I pretended to like girls when I was with my friends, perhaps afraid they'd hate me if they knew the truth, but I never really had a girlfriend. I mean sometimes, if one of my friends was dating a girl and she had a 'friend', they would kind of force us together, but it never went anywhere and it was never particularly comfortable."

"Ok, so, if you were never particularly comfortable with women, why are you questioning things now?"

"I don't know. Maybe a part of me is wondering if I am missing out on something," said Jason shrugging again as he scans the remaining scones on the table.

As I sat there watching him, I recalled my own adolescent years that so closely mirrored his own. After a short pause while he devoured yet another scone, Jason came out with something that I think he had wanted to ask me for a very long time but clearly had never plucked up enough courage…until now.

CHAPTER 8

"Mum says you weren't always gay, uncle. So, you must have switched lifestyles before, which one was better?"

"Aah," I said realizing what had been burning at the back of his mind. "Well, it's impossible to say and frankly I don't really consider I switched at all. I have never been one to be hooked on labels, and though I have always liked men, I still don't consider myself gay or bi-sexual, or that I had a straight life in the past and now I have switched to a gay life. I am just me, in the same way that you are just you. Gender really doesn't play as big a part in things for me, especially these days, as it is more about a person's energy that I am attracted to. Remember we are all spiritual beings having a temporary human existence, and therefore it is possible to find that energy connection you may be subconsciously seeking, in everyone no matter what gender they are or identify with in this life. However, it is true that for many years I was in a heterosexual, long-term relationship. Two in fact, not to mention various other attempts at dating women in between."

"Really? I am little confused. If you always liked men, how come you ended up with women?"

"There were a ton of reasons and justifications that I used to rationalize my thoughts and actions. I was young, younger than you are now actually, and I hadn't worked out at that stage what it was that I was searching for. So, I thought it was what I wanted at the time; I thought it was what was expected of me; I thought it was what my mother would want; I thought that dating a woman was socially more acceptable to friends and family. Like you just said, I thought life would be less complicated, and maybe, like a lost puppy, I just fell into a relationship when I suddenly found myself the target of someone who genuinely liked me and showed me some affection. A scratch under the chin or behind the ears does wonders for a puppy's loyalty!"

Jason giggled as I continued.

"The fact that this person happened to be a woman was no-never-mind. I must admit, I was also even more shy then, kind of scared in a big city like London, certainly inexperienced and never in and out of relationships like people seem to be these days. So, it was all a bit of a novelty for me."

"So, who was she?"

"Anna? Oh, she was lovely, and we got on very well. I went to work at a company as a temp, and basically, I was her boss,"

"She slept with the boss?"

"Yes, and office romances are not to be recommended either. I had to leave the company and go and work somewhere else because we were both full of the joys of a new romance. It soon became obvious that we weren't focusing on work and things were getting behind, but it was worth it. Being together was fun and within a few months, we moved in together. Possibly because it was also economically more sensible than living separately. Living in London was expensive and her rent was also about to go up…again. So, perhaps I leapt at the chance to be the knight riding up on a white horse to save the damsel in distress. Who knows. Whatever the reasons were, we very quickly became very good friends, and remained that way, even after we broke up."

"So how long were you together?"

"About 15 years. We rented several properties during that time until we eventually bought a house of our own. Life evolved into a very suburban lifestyle, complete with golf club membership, local friends and us hosting epic dinner parties. It really was a great time in my life," I said nostalgically.

"So, all that time you were with her you still liked men? Did she ever know or suspect?"

"I have no idea. You'd need to ask her that question, but it really doesn't matter now. It ran its course and eventually we split and went our separate ways."

"So, what happened after that?"

"Well, after a suitable amount of time licking wounds and letting the dust settle, I went back to dating and set up profiles on a range of websites to try to meet someone new. You must remember that online dating was still a relatively new thing in those days. Prior to that, the only dating service that existed, were dating agencies where you physically went to a place, completed a profile questionnaire and gave them a couple of snapshots."

"Really, did you ever go to one?"

Just then Mara appeared to tell us that dinner was ready. Admittedly we had planned an early dinner expecting Jason to be a little jetlagged from the flight, but I still couldn't believe we had been talking for so long and the time had just flown by.

"Yes, I did once, but that will have to wait until after dinner."

CHAPTER 9

Mara had prepared a delicious dinner for us, as always, but kept it simple thinking that anything too heavy might just send Jason straight off to sleep.

I had an outdoor 'dining pit' at the bottom of the garden overlooking the beach. It was basically a long picnic table and benches made from distressed driftwood, which had been sunken into the ground, thus providing some shelter from any sea breeze that might have sprung up. Fortunately, that evening, the ocean was calm with not a breath of wind nor a cloud in the sky.

While we had been talking, Mara had diligently prepared the table with everything we needed including a large array of candles and stacks of cushions to keep us comfortable. Paulo soon appeared and, after greeting Jason, the four of us settled down for a delicious dinner. Opting for a predominantly Mexican theme, Mara had prepared fajitas with a mixture of meats, side salads, homemade bread and her famous guacamole, washed down with a couple of beers for the boys. One of life's simple pleasures that I always enjoyed was watching the sun go down over a simple candlelit supper with those closest to me.

After dinner, we sat there and watched as the sky was slowly set ablaze with every shade of yellow, orange and red imaginable as the sun sank slowly into the ocean to end its fiery reign for another day. Of course, Jason was keen to get back to our earlier discussion.

"So, what was this story you were going to tell me earlier about going to a dating agency?"

"Oh that!" I chuckled as I took another swig of beer. "My best friend from school and I were about 19 at the time, I guess, and we got it into our heads that we weren't meeting enough or the right kind of women. To be honest, I wasn't meeting any at all for obvious reasons, but if I remember correctly, it was his idea, and he just talked me into going along with him for moral support. So, we made appointments to go and be interviewed and then promptly went up to the cemetery to try to take some up-to-date snapshots for our profiles."

"The cemetery?? Gross!"

"Hmmm, how romantic!?" chipped in Mara.

"It wasn't all that bad, and I think I still have the photos somewhere. Anyway, we duly had our interviews and paid our money, but it was a complete disaster. Ironically, looking back, I was the only one who got set up on a date. My friend, who was much better looking than me, didn't get a single sniff. So, one Friday evening, I got all dressed up, borrowed a company car from work, and as luck would have it, I was house sitting so I had a place to myself. Everything appeared to be perfect, stars seemed to be aligning, what could possibly go wrong I told myself."

"So, what happened?"

I chuckled and continued. "It was arranged that I would pick her up from work and we would go and have a drink and see how things went. When I got there, I spoke to some guy and said who I was. Then I sat at a table and waited and waited and waited. Well, it transpired that she either got cold feet, or took one look at me and thought naaah, and legged it out through the kitchen of the restaurant where she was working!"

It was Jason's turn to stifle a snigger at my expense as I took another swig of beer while Paulo and Mara fell about laughing.

"I couldn't even tell you what she looked like, though I may have caught a quick glimpse of her blond hair as she scarpered out the back door. Thankfully, after that, my friend seemed to lose interest in the idea and so ended our days of dating agencies."

"That's hilarious," said Jason.

"Of course, these days, if you don't fancy someone, you can just block them from the comfort of your own home while sitting on the sofa in your underwear. Obviously much more convenient, maybe too much so, and certainly far less dramatic, but not nearly as much of a giggle. I mean how many nights can you sit around a table with friends, drinking beers while regaling them with the time you got blocked by someone!?

"You guys sound a bit crazy to me, but you still went back to trying to date women after Anna?"

"Well, yeah sure. Don't forget, I had been in a straight relationship for most of my adult life, it had been a wonderful time so why not try to recreate it. Plus, it was really the only type of relationship I had ever known. Though I liked men, it never really entered my head to have a full-on relationship with a man. That's when I really started to realize how lucky I had been, being with Anna all those years, and how much it had sheltered me from the crazy people that I now know you can find everywhere."

"So, what sort of people did you meet?"

"Well, for example, there was The User, someone who turned up on the first date with her laptop because she thought she had a virus and all she wanted was free IT support while she went to buy me a beer."

"You're kidding" said Jason as they all giggled.

"The Liar, who knocked about 15 years off her age. I felt like I was having afternoon tea with one of my mother's friends. I am sure that must have been her Zimmer Frame parked outside that I tripped over on my way into the bar."

"What?"

"The Blocker, or maybe she was what they refer to as a bunny boiler, who perhaps thankfully I never got to meet because she messaged me whilst I was in the shower. As I failed to respond immediately, she then sent me another message which was nothing more than a tirade of abuse and promptly blocked me."

"Yikes" said Jason.

"See how lucky you are?!" said Mara as she turned to Paulo and poked him in the stomach with her finger.

"Then there was the Untrusting Man Hater, whom when I decided to buy her a bunch of flowers, asked me what she had done to deserve them. When I said 'nothing, I just thought you might like them', she leapt on me with what have *you* done that I deserve them!? As though they were some sort of guilt appeasing peace offering."

There were sniggers from all round the table once again.

"Go on," said Jason

"Then there was the Narcissist, who convinced me to go on a short break to northern Spain, simply because, as it turned out, she wanted an obliging chauffer. We did end up having sex on a hotel balcony late one afternoon as the sun was going down, which I admit was fun, in a rockstar kind of way! However, when I no longer served a purpose for her, she turned on me, screaming down the phone that I had a mental problem and needed to urgently be committed! Then threatened me with a restraining order should I ever try to contact her again!"

"Shit!" exclaimed Jason.

"All I said was 'hey, how you doing?' when I answered her phone call."

"No way!" exclaimed Jason. "It sounds like a catalogue of the guys I keep meeting."

"Yes, exactly. So, you see, it really doesn't matter what gender people are or how they identify themselves. If someone has no intention of treating you right, they won't, no matter who they are, and you can't control anyone else's actions no matter what you do. What many people, far smarter than me will tell you, and what I had to learn the hard way, is you always need to be true to yourself and put yourself first."

"Yeah, so my friends keep telling me." said Jason. "But didn't you say you had 2 long term relationships, who was the other one?

"Ah, that was Karen. She was the last woman I dated."

"Basically, I was planning on moving to Porto when we met. She said all the right things, and I thought it might be easier to move there as a couple, instead of on my own. So, we got together, and I moved in with her after a couple of months."

"After about 3 years of rubbing along, we bought an apartment in Porto and, as it turned out, moved there to ride out the Covid pandemic. Up until that point, things had been okay, I think mainly because we both liked to travel, and we travelled a lot."

"However, the pandemic ended all of that and we found ourselves sitting in our apartment in Porto, staring at each other. It turned out that she didn't like doing the things that I liked, and I didn't like doing the things she liked. So, in order not to upset each other, we ended up doing nothing."

"That was when it became apparent that, other than travel, we really had nothing in common, and it was just a matter of time before things would come to an end."

"So, what happened?" asked Jason.

"After a few months, once the covid restrictions began to ease, she went back to the UK, and I stayed in Porto. That was when my life got turned completely on its head.

Really? Said Jason stifling a yawn.

"Yeah, but it is getting late, and I can see you are flagging, so we'll save that for tomorrow."

Jason agreed that the flight was catching up with him, so we said good night, and he headed off to bed.

CHAPTER 10

I helped Mara clear away the remnants of dinner and then headed off to my own private lounge area in the master suite. It was still early for me so I thought I would read for a bit but couldn't get back into the book. Simply mentioning the life-changing moment that I would relate to Jason the next day left me suddenly, and uncontrollably, reminiscing about Francisco.

As I sat there on my double facing sofas, surrounded by the same beige and chocolate colored scatter cushions as the outdoor lounging area, and gently massaging the soles of my feet in the thick shag pile rug that lined the entire seating area, I sighed, and gave up trying to read. I marked my page again and gently threw the book onto an identical glass-topped coffee table, just like the one in the outdoor seating area, with a clunk, and swung my legs up onto the sofa. I gazed out over the koi pond that bordered the front of the master suite, across the garden, between the palm trees and out to the now dark black ocean beyond, where there was nothing but the twinkling of cabin lights on various pleasure boats that seemed to mirror the twinkling stars in the sky. I closed my eyes and let my mind drift back to that pivotal day when Francisco and I first met.

It wasn't long after the covid pandemic restrictions had started to lift in Portugal and Karen had decided to go back to the UK. Having sat around for the better part of two years with little to no socializing I decided I would take the opportunity, of being on my own, to try to meet some new people and expand my social circle. What a good plan I thought. However, there was a nagging idea, a curiosity if you will, that had been lurking in the back of my mind for longer than I care to remember. Perhaps I'll download Grindr and just have a little peek and see what sort of guys are on it, I mean…just to look.

It wasn't long before this guy messaged me and asked if I wanted to meet for a drink. A harmless drink, I told myself and who knows I might make a new friend, after all, expanding my social circle was what I was all about. Yes, covid pandemic restrictions had started to lift, but bars were still closed at this point and there was nowhere to get a drink without a meal as well. Oh well, I thought. Let's just see what happens.

We arranged to meet at the base of Pont Luis I Bridge at 6:00pm. As it was March, it was already dark and there was a slight chill in the air as it had been raining. The streets were dimly lit and only a few people were out and about. I dutifully waited at the predetermined location and soon, this tall figure walked across the street and headed towards me. As he approached, he flashed a smile and introduced himself as Francisco. We exchanged pleasantries and then he suggested we get a drink.

Looking around at the various bars that lined the north side of the river, I said, "Ok, but I have no idea where, everything seems to be closed."

"Yes, you're right," he agreed. Then, after a moment's pause, he said he had some wine back at his place and suggested we could go there.

Looking at him in the dim light, I wasn't all that comfortable with the idea, but I was also reasonably confident from his energy that he wasn't an axe murderer either, so I agreed and off we walked.

It took about 10 minutes to get to his place, all the while we casually chatted, between pants for breath, as we scaled the hills in Porto's Ribeira district. By the time we got to his place, I was feeling a little more relaxed and as we entered, I discovered he was renting a beautiful, newly refurbished apartment. It was ground floor with a couple of steps down into a kitchen area which extended into a small dining cum living room with a door that led to the bedroom and ensuite bathroom at the back. The entire place was tastefully decorated in polar white and soft grey coloring and was spotlessly clean and tidy. The recessed spotlights cast soft lighting around the slightly masculine decor and, having been invited to sit, I instantly made myself comfortable on the sofa.

Francisco opened a bottle of wine, poured a couple of glasses then came and sat with me. Though I had seen his photos online, I was now able, for the first time, to get a good look at him and was surprised by how much younger he was than me. He had a pleasant, slightly round, baby face with a closely cropped beard and moustache and short trimmed hair that was already slightly receding. He had a wonderfully warm smile and dark brown eyes that twinkled behind rimless glasses.

He was very gentle, intelligent and extremely charming, and though English was not his first language, it was far better than my Portuguese. Getting lost in his seductive accent, I quickly became oblivious to the passing of time as we sat, talked and laughed our way through not one, but 2 bottles of wine. As we emptied our glasses for the last time, Francisco made his move. After taking my glass and placing it on the side table behind him, he reached over, gently took my face in his hands, passionately kissed me…oh wow, how he could kiss…and I melted right there on the spot!

When I was younger, I had my fair share of experiences with men, but they were just anonymous hookups and kissing was never really a part of it. Of course, I kissed my female partners throughout our relationships, but this was something completely different. This was sensual yet masculine, gentle yet passionate all at the same time and tasted of the wine we had been drinking all evening. The more he kissed me, the more I melted, as did any remaining reservations that I may have been harboring.

After a short time, we moved into the bedroom and quietly undressed to get into bed. As I watched him, my jaw dropped as he slowly revealed, bit by bit, the most amazing, 6 foot one, olive skinned, Brazilian body of a god I had ever seen. Frightened I was going to wake up any minute to find this was all a figment of my imagination, I eagerly climbed into bed with him. We spent hours exploring, playing and enjoying each other until inevitably we both came, before finally curling up and falling asleep together. It was the first time I had spent the entire night in another man's arms, and it was a whole new world for me.

All too soon, morning arrived, his alarm went off and I quickly dressed to leave, but he wouldn't let me go. Not before he made me breakfast and coffee, which was so sweet. By the time came for me to go home, and him off to work, I was completely hooked and I knew my life would never be the same again.

    Suddenly a cool ocean breeze caused me to shudder and brought me back from my indulgent trip down memory lane. Once again, sitting on my sofa with half-closed, dreamy eyes and a wistful yet contented smile on my face, I let my awareness return to my surroundings before deciding it really had been a long day. I stood and shuddered from another gust of cool wind as I slowly took myself off to bed.

CHAPTER 11

It was another glorious morning as I awoke to the tranquil sounds of the crystal-clear turquoise waters lapping the shore and the sea breeze gently rustling the palm trees of my beach front villa. Looking around me and feeling more like Bill Murray in Groundhog Day, I let out a sigh of resignation as I slid over to the edge of the bed and began that all too familiar morning routine.

As I sat there, hanging my head with my eyes closed, his face appeared once again in my mind's eye. For a moment, I wondered how he was and hoped he was happy, whilst remembering his dark brown eyes, like two pools of melted chocolate, and his unbelievable smile. I wiped away a small tear that was clinging to my eyelash, like that first drop of melted snow that clings to the tip of a pine tree branch, and sparkles with the first rays of the early morning light. Hauling my weary ass, and my heavy heart, up off the bed, I headed for the shower.

After a time, once I was suitably together again and ready to face the world, I headed over to the kitchen, desperately in need of coffee, but as I approached, I suddenly stopped dead in my tracks. No!!!! Surely not….it can't be…can it!?

Like a cartoon character being dragged along on tip toes by his nose, which was twitching madly with a mind of its own, I followed the delicious, familiar and intoxicating smell. As I rounded the corner, I saw Mara standing over a frying pan full of bacon and black pudding.

"Good morning!" said Mara in her normal jovial self.

"Huh?...What? Oh…yeah…good morning"

"Did you sle…"

"Is that Stornoway Black Pudding?" I asked as I pointed rather rudely at the frying pan.

"Yes! I thought it might cheer you up a bit"

"Where on earth did you get it? It is impossible to find here"

Mara slapped my hand with the spatula as I tried to steal a small morsel of black pudding that had broken off in the pan.

"I have my sources but the less you know the better. I had to pay a small King's ransom for it, but I figured it would be worth it for you and Jason."

"Who?" I asked not taking my eyes off the frying pan for even a second. "Oh, yeah Jason. Have you seen him this morning?"

"No, not yet. Poor boy must be exhausted. Better let him sleep."

"Yeah, I'll just look after his Black Pud…"

"You'll do no such thing! I know you too well, so I have Jason's share stashed away where you can't get it!"

With that, Mara presented me with a plate, filled with a glorious Full English Breakfast, and a large mug of builders' tea.

As I took the biggest breath my poor old lungs could handle and savored every delicious aroma wafting up from my plate, I thanked Mara profusely and exclaimed that I had no idea what I would do without her.

"Starve, most likely!"

"Mmm" was the closest thing Mara would get to me conceding she was probably right as I tucked into my breakfast, swimming in all the delightful tastes and textures that you can only get from a fat boy's breakfast!

Having finished everything on my plate, I sat there for a few minutes, stuffed like the proverbial Strasbourg Goose, and thanked Mara again as she cleared my plate away. With still no sign of Jason, I grabbed a fresh mug of tea and staggered off to my office.

CHAPTER 12

I settled into my normal routine and had no sooner finished with my daily accounting chores, when WhatsApp on my phone buzzed. It was my old friend Mel.

Mel was a former colleague who was a couple of years younger than me, and we worked together almost 2 decades ago in London. Blimey…how time flies! I only worked there for 5 months but we instantly became very good friends and stayed in touch after I left. We often spoke once or twice a week and, occasionally, even headed off on holiday together. We had always been there for each other, and no matter how often we spoke, one of us always had some ongoing drama to share with the other.

Lately, Mel had been having a bit of a tough time with various aspects of her life. Well, this seemed to be more of an ongoing state of affairs. If it wasn't one thing, it was another.

"Well, hey! … A very good morning to you too! How ya doing? … No, you're not disturbing me. I'm not really doing anything at the moment, just my normal day-to-day stuff. … Uh oh, what's happened? … Really? … Oh, you gotta be kidding me! … And then what happened? … No way! What did he say?"

Just then, Jason appeared in the doorway of my office. With glass walls, there was never any need for anyone to knock. I motioned to him to come in and sit on the sofa, so he stepped in and slumped down, looking decidedly uncomfortable.

"Of course, you can come and stay for a while if you need to get away. There's always a space here for you, you know that! … Whenever suits you. I have no plans to go anywhere for the next few weeks. … My nephew Jason is staying with me for a while so, if she is ok with that, then of course she can come too if she wants. You know there is plenty of room. ... Ok, well, go and check out flights, then let me know which one you'll be on, and I'll meet you at the airport. ... Ok. Speak later. ... Bye!"

I put the phone down and turned my attention to Jason. "Judging by the look on your face, I assume you have just finished breakfast with Mara," I smiled.

"Oh god yeah, it was amazing, but I seriously struggled to move afterwards. How I made it this far is anyone's guess," he chuckled.

"So, what's on the agenda for today then?"

"Probably nothing until I have digested some of that breakfast"

"I know how you feel. Mara keeps us so well fed it's a miracle I am not the size of a house."

There was a short pause as I turned my attention back to my computer, but I could sense Jason was dying to ask me something.

"So, what was it that turned your life upside down that you were going to tell me about?" Jason eventually asked.

"Well, it wasn't so much as what but who. His name was Francisco. A 32-year-old Brazilian with the body of a god!"

Fresh from last night's trip down memory lane, I retold the story to Jason of how we met.

"It was a whole new world that had opened up to me. One in which I had only ever dared to dip my toe in up to that point. However, I instinctively knew, from that day on, it would be unlikely that I would ever look to date a woman again."

"Wow! Was he really that amazing?" asked Jason with raised eyebrows.

"Oh yeah!"

"So, what happened?"

"Well, I am not completely clear on his reasons, but basically, he didn't want to have any sort of serious relationship. All he wanted was a fuck buddy. Someone he could meet up with regularly and have some fun with, without any attachments. He was open and upfront with me about this right from the start."

"What did you say?"

"Oh, I was fine with it. I certainly wasn't going to turn down the chance to be with someone like him. You must understand, I was already over 50 at that point and super grateful that he had a thing for daddies."

Jason just smiled, knowingly and quietly chuckled.

"So, we started seeing each other once a week, usually on a Friday evening. He'd come over and we'd sit out on the terrace overlooking the city. We'd talk and laugh and generally hangout while we downed a couple of bottles of wine before heading to bed for a long, and I mean long, sex session"

"Really? He was good?" said Jason suddenly showing more interest.

"Oh...he was more than good! It was, without a doubt, the best sex I have ever had in my life."

"Including both men and women?"

"Yes. Including everyone I have ever had sex with. He was playful and fun, yet sensual and caring. Dominant and so very masculine yet at the same time tender and gentle."

I sat staring into space for a moment, my mind recalling every smile on his face, every muscular ripple of his body. "We had so much fun," I sighed wistfully.

"Go on," said Jason now suddenly more alert than before.

"I remember, my Portuguese still wasn't that great, so he kind of became my teacher and would help me practice. I don't know what made me do it, but one day I decided to make up a story and translate it into Portuguese as I thought it would be good practice. However, thinking about him and the incredible sex we were having, it ended up becoming an erotic adult story. One where he was the handsomest teacher in all the city, and I was the errant student who didn't do his homework. The kid at the back of the class who was never focused on the lesson as he was always off on some sexual fantasy with his gorgeous teacher."

"And then what did you do?" chuckled Jason.

"Well, once I had translated it, I would spend the rest of the week memorizing it, so when he came over on Friday, I could snuggle up to him wherever we were, on the terrace, curled up on the sofa, or even just standing in the kitchen while we drank our wine, and whisper it into his ear, like it was a secret fantasy."

"How did he react?"

"How do you think??!! It turned him on so much, that I never got to the end of the story before he'd rip his jeans off revealing he had come commando to my place, and we'd start the night's gymnastics right there."

"No way! Even in the kitchen?" exclaimed Jason.

"I kid you not! Each week I had to come up with a new chapter, and I tell you what, my Portuguese improved no end!"

I chuckled a little as I paused again for a moment thinking to myself. "It really was another amazing time in my life. I remember this one weekend when spending time with him and the sex was extraordinarily good, that it was the following Wednesday before I realized the clocks had gone forward that weekend!"

"You're kidding!"

"No. I was on such a cloud nine high that I was completely oblivious to the entire world around me."

"Wow. I can't even begin to imagine what that must have been like."

"Hmm. It was truly amazing…as was he. Come on," I said, coming back to the present moment. "I think I need a cup of tea, and I better warn Mara and Paulo that Mel and her friend are coming to stay. You remember Mel, don't you?"

"Yeah, I think so. When are they coming?"

"I am not sure yet but probably at the end of the week."

With that we got up and headed off to the kitchen.

CHAPTER 13

It was another glorious day and far too nice to be sitting in the office chatting, so we took our tea and sat at the edge of the pool. The temperature was quickly rising as the day wore on and it felt wonderful dangling our feet in the cool water as I continued the story of Francisco from where I had left off.

"The apartment I was living in was wonderful. It was built sometime in the 1920's and over the years the building had moved and settled and so there were some quirky features such as the floor slopping, very noticeably, from one side to the other. Sometimes It almost felt like you were walking up hill to get to the dining table. Another quirk was that hardly any of the internal doors closed, including the door of the master bedroom. They simply didn't align with the door frames anymore."

"That would feel a bit strange, not being able to have any privacy," said Jason.

"Well, I wasn't sharing the place with anyone, so what did it matter."

"Yeah, I guess"

"Anyway, Friday nights had developed their own routine. It would be drinks, then eventually off to bed for some amazing sex, sleep, and then in the morning we invariably had round two, before showering and him heading off home. Leaving me basking in the glow of all that had transpired until Friday came round again.

I looked at Jason and he was just slightly smiling and nodding, again in a knowing fashion.

"Anyway, I remember this one weekend, we had probably slept too long so by the time round 2 came and went, the world was awake and getting on with its day."

"What happened?"

"Well, we were talking afterwards while we both recovered from the exertion, if you know what I mean, and Francisco was complaining that his legs were sore as he had done a leg workout the previous day. So, being ever helpful, I went to the bathroom, retrieved some massage oil and started to give his thighs a bit of a sports massage."

"Hmm, nice!"

"So, I was rubbing my hands up and down his gorgeous thighs trying to get his muscles to relax a bit. Only, he wasn't really relaxing was he! Needless to say, it wasn't very long at all before he was getting aroused again and I thought…hmm…round three?! So, I moved a little further up the bed so I could reach him, I mean how could I resist! Then, no sooner had I taken his cock in my hands and was about to go down on him, there was a sudden and very loud knock at the front door."

Jason started to giggle.

"Startled, we looked at each other, panic in Francisco's eyes as though we had been caught and in a frantic whisper asking what he should do. 'Nothing.' I quietly replied. 'Just stay here and keep quiet,' as I threw on some sweats. 'At least close the door!' Francisco insisted in a pleading whisper whilst indicating the bedroom door. 'I can't, they don't close anymore. Don't worry, I'm not going to let anyone in.' With that, I made my way to the front door and as I turned the corner of the hallway, I looked back to see Francisco, lying there on his back in all his naked glory, his legs slightly parted, thighs glistening with oil, with this huge erection and a look of dread across his face."

Jason was now in fits of laughter. "So, who was at the door."

"It was my neighbor from upstairs who had come down to offer me some pot plants, which she had been splitting out from her window boxes. Never before had she ever offered me anything like this and I knew, instantly, it was just a thinly veiled rouse. It was clear that because we had overslept, they must have been having breakfast or something upstairs and had heard us having round 2. So, she had come down to be nosey."

"What happened then?"

"Sadly, nothing. I managed to get rid of the nosey neighbor and returned to the room to find the whole ordeal had deflated poor Francisco and round 3 never eventuated. We just showered, dressed, had some coffee and he went home."

CHAPTER 14

"So, what happened to him?"

I sat there again, wistfully staring into the pool for a moment. "It ended not long afterwards. It was my fault. I ruined it."

"How?"

"He was totally upfront with me about his expectations and what he wanted as I said, and even though I was ok with it, the more time I spent with him, the more I got to know him. The more I got to know him, the more I realized what a wonderful person he was. Not only was he gorgeous and amazing in bed, but he was also very intelligent, well read, a good conversationalist and really funny. He was the whole package, and I ended up falling in love with him," I shrugged. "Eventually, I guess he felt my deepening feelings for him, so he took me out to a bar down by the river late one afternoon, the only time we ever went anywhere in public together, and he ended it."

"That must have been hard."

"Oh, I was devasted! I think my reaction was worse than he anticipated. He tried to soften things by saying we could still be friends, but I knew it was never going to happen."

I paused again looking distantly into the waters of the pool as the moment replayed in my mind.

"Anyway, we finished our drinks and eventually headed toward the Pont Luis I Bridge. The place where we had first met, which had a kind of symmetry about it, until our paths diverged and he left me, literally, crying in the street."

"Oh my god! What did you do???"

"There was nothing I could do, other than watch him walk away, round a corner, and disappear from my life. I stood there for a few moments, hoping he might reemerge, but he didn't. I looked around me not knowing what else to do. With my head spinning like a whirlwind, I managed to walk to the nearest bus stop where I sat for about an hour and a half and just cried and cried, openly in public. I didn't even know where I was anymore. I didn't know where to go, who to talk to, nothing. Buses would pull up but I didn't have any idea where they were going, so I just sat there. The drivers would look at me for a minute or two, then close the doors and drive off. It felt as though my entire world had collapsed, and I was struggling to even breathe."

"Wow! Did you ever speak to him again?"

"Not really. He messaged me a couple of times while I was sitting at the bus stop to see if I was ok. I am sure he must have felt bad seeing me so devasted and I am certain he never meant to hurt me. Looking back, it was like I was 18 years old again and I had just lost the first love of my life, but after that, I never heard from him again."

"That really must have hurt!"

"Yeah, it took me about a year to get over him. To stop tearing up every time I thought of him, which was often." I heaved a sigh and continued. "Eventually the wound healed, but I knew he had changed my life forever."

"How? Wasn't he just a fuck buddy in the end?"

"No, to me he was so much more than that. He was a watershed moment in my life."

"Huh?"

I paused, looking out to sea as I gathered my thoughts for a minute.

"I don't know exactly when it started, but for as far back as I can remember, I always had this special place where I kept all my deepest, darkest secrets. I am sure most people can relate to having something similar."

"Yeah, I know I certainly do."

"So, as the years went by and life experiences came and went, I would add more and more secrets. The place then kind of expanded from a chest to a vault and so on, until it soon became like a castle in my mind. Every time someone got close to getting in there, I would strengthen the battlements to protect it. I started to build walls around it to keep people out. A series of concentric circular spaces surrounding my fortification. Depending on who you were, and the level of trust I felt with you, determined which level you'd be allowed to have access to. Strangers were never allowed in at all, period! Then there was a layer for acquaintances, another for friends and family, and then one for close friends, lovers, partners and so on. Each one getting progressively closer to my castle of secrets. However, no one ever gained access to the castle. That was off limits to the entire world."

"Until you met Francisco, right?"

"Yeah, and the effect of him was devastating. Not only did he succeed in gaining access to the castle, but as we broke up, he basically bulldozed the whole thing, the castle, the walls everything. Not intentionally of course…I am sure he had no idea. But once he was gone, I felt like I was left sitting there, surrounded by nothing more than a pile of rubble. For the first time in my life, I felt completely vulnerable and totally exposed to the whole world."

"Wow," whispered Jason.

"My friends became concerned because, obviously, my mood changed. I was heartbroken, sad and crying a lot but with nowhere to retreat to. No safe haven where I could I hide and lick my wounds."

"So, what did you do?"

"One by one, I started telling my friends and those closest to me what had happened. I guess I was kind of reaching out to them for the support I needed at the time."

"So, you basically started coming out to people?"

"Yep. Not an easy thing to do as I am sure most people who have come out will attest to and certainly not an easy thing to do in your 50's when you have spent your entire adult life living a completely different lifestyle."

"So, you were living a lie?"

"I'm not sure I would call it that necessarily, but I certainly wasn't being true to certain aspects of my life and primarily who I really was."

"Hmm" mused Jason.

"Yeah, so you see, getting back to your question from yesterday, it really doesn't matter what lifestyle you choose. It is better to be who you are and follow the path that is right for you."

CHAPTER 15

I HAD NO IDEA WHAT DISTURBED ME FROM MY SLEEP THE NEXT MORNING. We lived at the end of the beach with hardly any neighbors, and virtually no noise, other than the sounds of nature that surrounded us. However, I suddenly awoke and noticed it was barely daybreak. As I slowly became aware of my physical surroundings, I quickly realized that this was a very special morning, one that doesn't happen terribly often. Dispensing with my normal routine, I climbed out of bed, threw on my shorts and a T-shirt, grabbed a sweatshirt and headed off to the kitchen.

I scribbled a note for Mara saying I wouldn't be needing breakfast this morning, that I was going out for a walk on the beach and not to worry. I then grabbed an apple from the fruit bowl and headed out.

I passed the outdoor seating area, took the path down the left side of the pool and soon came to the gate at the bottom of the garden, which leads directly onto the beach. Quietly letting myself out, I disappeared into the early morning light.

I walked along the beach, paddling my feet in the crystal-clear water's edge like I normally do. Often, I take my ear buds with me and do a walking-meditation. It's excellent for clearing the head, and I find Colette Baron-Reid's 11-minute meditations, are perfect to get me most of the way to the far end. However, today I chose to walk in silence, lost in my own thoughts. Feeling the cool ocean as it gently licked at my ankles and then scurried away, like a boisterous child intent on luring me into a game of tag.

As it was still early, only a few people were out and about. Most of them were probably American tourists who come here and rent accommodation in one of the beach front properties, including my own.

You can always tell, as they're usually the ones on the beach from early morning until sunset. Soaking in as much paradise as they can during their annual 2-week vacation, before heading back, often to their over-worked, over-stressed and probably under-paid jobs. Invariably chained to a desk in a glass, high-rise monstrosity in the middle of a noisy, polluted city. My imagination runs away with me, and I conjure an image of them leading a miserable life, similar to that of the guy sentenced to 40 years in the state penitentiary, whose only escape from doing his penance, is exercising in the yard for 1 hour a day.

Occasionally I'll stop and chat with them. It's interesting how they all say the same thing when I suggest they should move somewhere near a beach if they love the beach so much. They tell me they prefer life in the city and would miss it terribly if they were to leave. They love the excitement, the buzz and the pace of life. They seem so passionate about how they can feel the pulse of the city, as they fight their way through the hustle and bustle to the office every morning, stopping only to grab their onion bagel and coffee on the way.

The cynical part of me can't help but ponder if it is the pulse of the city they are feeling, or their own adrenaline, and dangerously elevated blood pressure, from living in the middle of that rat race. A pressure that could be surging them closer to their next heart attack with every beat of the very heart that could fail on them at any given moment!

I also wonder why they come here, if they love the city so much, and spend almost every waking moment sucking up as much sun, sand and sea breeze as they possibly can. Just like a terrified patient in the dentist's chair, desperately inhaling every last waft of Novocain their poor lungs handle, because the fear of the ensuing pain is just too much to bear.

However, I park my imagination into neutral, bite my tongue and say nothing. I just nod sagely, concede it's no longer the life for me, and continue on my way.

Most of the time, when I am out walking, I stop at the Beach Club towards the far end of the beach. It is a private members' club complete with sports facilities, tennis courts and a swimming pool, as well as various bars and restaurants. Being a property owner, my household is entitled to free membership, as are all the residents along the beach, and I'll often bump into neighbors there late in the afternoon. Many of them are supposed to be out walking their dogs, but instead, are sucking on the straw of a Tom Collins in one of the beach cabanas, whilst their dogs are laying glum faced under the table. All the dogs know me and are instantly on their feet with tails wagging, looking for cuddles and a scratch behind their ears, whenever I walk in. I love it! It is such a great buzz being part of this community and, because I don't have a dog of my own, all their dogs are very special to me.

However, this was a special day as there was not a breath of wind, and the ocean was as calm as a mill pond. Seemingly like I was on some sort of mission, I did not stop or talk with anyone, nor did I stop at the Beach Club, but instead continued to the very end of the beach where the bay curved out towards the sea like some giant fishhook laying on its side. Here at the end of the beach was a special place for me. I sat on the rocks and looked out to where there was a reef poking up through the surface of the water, about 100 meters out from the headland, where I was sitting.

Those who know me know I can often be found here, but very few understand why. Aside from the odd bird fluttering about in the trees nearby, there was barely a sound. The distinct smell of salt from the ocean mingled with the decaying seaweed trapped in the rock pools all around me and assaulted my nostrils with every breath. It was acrid and slightly offensive, but after a few moments, I became accustomed to it, and then it seemed to become almost familiar and even comforting.

To the untrained eye, I was just sitting motionless, staring out at the ocean like some bereft person waiting in vain for their lost lover to return from the sea. Everything around me was as still as could be. There weren't even any waves breaking on the shore, just the gentle lapping of the cool waters as they caressed the rocks, and the sand that bound them together.

As I sat there and watched the ocean, while listening to the sound of my own breath as my chest rose and fell in hypnotic rhythm, I closed my eyes, and I was immediately transported back to him. Back to those many nights when I would lay in the dark with my head resting on his chest. Feeling the warmth of his body beneath my head as I gently pressed my cheek into the soft hairs of his toned torso. Most of the time

I had no idea if he was awake or not. The only certainty was that same rhythmical rising and falling of his chest under my head and the ever-constant beating of his heart.

I hardly ever slept when I was with him. It was such a wonderful experience that I didn't want to miss it by sleeping. I would just drink in every moment, savor every cuddle when he wrapped his arms around me and sensuously played with my fingertips beneath the pillow supporting my head. Then we would roll over, changing positions as people do, and I'd just lay there watching him as he slept wrapped in my arms.

They say that when people sleep, generally, all their defenses are down and the masks they wear by day, drop away. They say that is when you can see who that person really is. They say if you look hard enough, you can see deep inside their heart and maybe even deep into their soul. That was how it was for me. Every time he slept, I could see deep into his heart and what an amazing heart he had. It radiated with so much energy it was like a galaxy of a million stars. The same stars that sparkled in his eyes when he was awake and radiated out through his smile. A smile that could melt steel.

If it were possible, I would have reached inside his chest, carefully scooped up his heart and placed it next to my own so they could beat together in unison for all eternity. These were the few, rare moments in my life when I felt the most profound sense of utter bliss and pure, unadulterated joy.

At times, if I listened intently enough, I felt as though I could hear the gentle whispers of the universe echoing in his chest in the same way you can hear the ocean when you hold a seashell up to your ear. It was the closest I believe I ever got to heaven in this lifetime and why I always said the world disappeared whenever I was in his arms.

"Uncle?"

"Uncle Charlie?!"

A distant voice suddenly brought me back to sitting on the rocks again. I had no idea how long I had been sitting there, but my ass was numb and Jason, who had come to find me was standing over me with a concerned hand resting gently on my shoulder. I wasn't even aware that he knew where to find me.

"Are you ok?"

"Huh…hmmm…what? Oh yes, hi Jason. Umm…I'm fine."

"Really you don't look fine. You look as though have been crying?"

"Oh…no…it's nothing, just salt from the ocean making my eyes water." I said as I wiped my eyes and regained my composure. "Here, come sit down. I want to show you something amazing that you have probably never seen before."

As Jason sat down, I tried to shuffle my position, not just to make room for him, but also to try to get some of the blood circulating in my butt again!

"Now, make sure you are sitting comfortably, clear you mind and look out to the reef just off the headland."

"Ok"

"Notice how the ocean gently rises and falls in relation to the rocks?"

"Yes"

"This happens all the time but is only noticeable under certain conditions like today when there isn't any wind to whip up the waves, the tide is low, and the ocean is as calm as a mill pond."

"Oh, ok"

"You've heard people suggest that the oceans are the lungs of the planet, right?"

"Yeah" said Jason hesitantly, unsure where I was heading with this.

"So, watch closely and feel the rhythm of the ocean as it gently rises and falls in relation to the rocks. Does it remind you of anything?"

After a brief moment Jason exclaimed, "Oh wow! It's like the ocean is breathing!"

"Exactly! But we don't normally notice it because waves do not always follow the same pattern when they break over the rocks and thus hide the rhythmical motion.

"That's amazing! It's like the whole planet is a massive, breathing, living thing!"

"Yep. Ok, now I want you to concentrate on the rhythm and get a real feel for it. Watch it's every movement as it goes up and then down again."

"OK"

"Got it?"

"Yeah, I think so."

"Good! Now what I want you to do is bring your attention to your own breathing as you continue to watch the rhythmic motion of the ocean and regulate your breathing, so you are breathing in the same rhythmic pattern."

"Ok"

"Breathe in as the water rises and breathe out as it drops. Again, breathe in as the water rises and then, out.

"Ok"

"As you continue and get that rhythm going, how do you feel?"

"Connected! Oh my god! It's like I am breathing in time with the ocean! It's like we are both breathing the same air and feeling the same energy! Wow!! That's incredible!"

I just sat there with a slight knowing smile on my face.

"I feel so small compared to the breathing of the planet, yet I also feel like I am part of every breath, part of something much bigger."

I said nothing…I just let Jason absorb things for a bit.

"So, this is why you come here?"

"Yes. It is one of the easiest and best mindfulness exercises I know of. The whole world disappears when I am here on days like this. It reminds me of other things and transports me to another time, another place."

"That's why you didn't notice me when I walked up to you?"

"Yes, I guess I was kind of meditating."

There was a long pause before Jason gently asked, "Is that why you appeared to have been crying?"

"Hmm" was all I muttered.

There was another pause as Jason seemed to be debating with himself as to whether he should ask or not, but curiosity got the better of him.

"Who was it?"

I said nothing…I just continued to stare out at the reef and the ocean beyond for a time.

"No one," I finally said with a sigh. "Just a brief shooting star. Come on, lets head back and see if we can get some breakfast at the Beach Club."

CHAPTER 16

We made our way to the Beach Club. As soon as we arrived, George, the head waiter, rushed over to greet us. George was a native of the island and had worked at the Beach Club for longer than any of the residents had been members. He was very attentive and always with a warm, welcoming smile as his perfectly white teeth flashed in contrast to his much darker tanned skin.

"Good morning, Mister Charlie" he almost sang, "It is a pleasure to see you, as always, on such a magnificent day."

We lived on a tropical Caribbean Island where most days were magnificent, but somehow, George had a way of making each one feel special and unique.

"Good morning, George, how are you?"

"Oh, just fine sir, thank you so much for asking."

"You remember my nephew Jason, don't you?" as I gestured towards my nephew.

"But of course!" said George bowing almost as though he was some forgotten relic from the days of the Raj in India. "It is a pleasure to welcome you once again to our wonderful Beach Club, Mister Jason. Now, what can I get you both?"

As we talked with George, we settled into one of the cabanas facing the beach. It was comprised of a central table and sumptuously padded sofa seating. This was surrounded by a four-poster frame, complete with a fabric roof and side curtains, which were tied to the posts in luxurious billowing folds of fabric. The whole thing looked more like some Bedouin tent that wouldn't be amiss in a stage production of Lawrence of Arabia.

"We'd like a couple Cappuccinos, some fresh orange juice and is there any chance of someone being able to rustle up a couple of breakfast rolls with egg and bacon?"

"Yes, of course. No problem at all!" said George before he turned and scurried away to get our order.

We sat for a moment in silence, but I could feel Jason wanting to pursue the conversation we were having while sitting on the rocks, however, I decided to divert him by changing the subject and asked him how he was enjoying living in Paris, one of the most romantic cities in the world.

"Oh, it's amazing and, of course, living in Saint Germain des Pres is such a bonus. All my friends are super jealous of the apartment."

I still owned an apartment in Paris but, as I hardly went there anymore, I let Jason move in and use it, basically, rent free. One of the many perks of being the favorite nephew of a wealthy, gay uncle who has no direct descendants sucking up his fortune.

"Good, I am glad you're enjoying yourself."

"Do you miss Paris at all?"

"Of course! Paris is one of the greatest cities I have ever lived in."

"What do you miss most about Paris"

"There are so many things, from Sacre Coeur, The Seine and Notre Dame to little back street bistros. Like most people I had my favorites that I used to go to."

"Yeah, me too."

"However, if I had to pick one thing, it would have to be the Eiffel Tower."

"Really? Why?"

"It is iconic. Completed on 31st March 1889 for the World's Fair in Paris, the Eiffel Tower wasn't exactly everyone's cup of tea. Many scholars, artists and influential people of the time were highly critical of what they considered to be an eyesore, a blot on the landscape, during its construction. However, once completed people slowly started to change their tune as it stood there, the tallest structure in the world for 41 years until it was eclipsed by the Chrysler Building in New York."

"Really?! With all the tall buildings in the world these days, I had no idea there was a time when the Eiffel Tower was the tallest structure in the world."

"Yes, but there were times when it nearly didn't survive. Once when it was under threat of being dismantled, its position on the Parisian skyline was, again, assured when Citroen rented the tower as an advertising space and created what, at that time was the world's largest advertisement, by having the word Citroen emblazoned vertically on three sides of its façade."

"Seriously? I can't even begin to imagine that!"

"Yes. 250,000 lightbulbs spelt out the name Citroen, the French car maker, from top to bottom and was so bright it could be seen from 60 miles away, I believe"

Just then George reappeared with our breakfast. "Here we are gentlemen, two breakfast rolls, orange juice and cappuccinos. Will that be all Mister Charlie?"

"Yes. Thank you, George."

"Very good sir" said George as he politely nodded and slipped away to tend to his other customers that were slowly filling the tables all around us.

"This looks delicious. I didn't realize how hungry I was" said Jason as we tucked into our breakfast.

We ate in silence for a moment, my mind still thinking about the significance of the Eiffel Tower before I picked up the conversation again.

"Of course, there is so much more to the Eiffel Tower than just an advertising hoarding. Imagine, she has stood, stoically, guarding over the city and people of Paris during not one but 2 world wars. She has borne witness to some of the worst atrocities of humanity during the 20th century that were taking place all around her. Her radio communications installations played a major part in jamming German radio signals as well as being instrumental in intercepting transmissions that led to the trial and execution of the infamous spy, Mata Hari."

"Seriously?"

"Yes. All the while she stood there, almost defiantly, as a beacon of hope for the people of Paris, steadfast, the embodiment of all things Parisian. Almost as if she were the guardian of the French Spirit and Culture during times when France was occupied by German forces who seemed determined to strip the country, and particularly Paris, of its cultural treasures."

Having scoffed his breakfast, Jason just sat there in silence, staring at me, almost hanging on every word, while I seemed to be reminiscing in a time long forgotten.

"Nowadays, despite her controversial beginnings, The Eiffel Tower is now one of the most popular tourist attractions in the world and synonymous with all things Parisian. I mean, can you even begin to imagine Paris without the Eiffel Tower?"

"No, not really, but I had never really considered it to be anything more than just a metal structure."

"Most people don't. They are too busy caught up in their own lives and possibly scurrying from one Parisian attraction to another during their far too brief stay in the city. You're lucky living in Paris as you have all the time in the world. So, next time, go and stand there or sit in one of the parks nearby and just watch what happens around you. You'll see that she now brings joy to millions of people from all over the world. If you watch you will hopefully notice that everyone you can see is happy and smiling, virtually no one is angry, sad or depressed despite whatever is going on in the world. Look at the families that come to visit. See the smiles on the faces of the parents as they show this marvel of engineering to their children who stand there, awestruck as their young minds try to take in the enormity of the structure they see before them. Look at the lovers, who stroll by holding hands. They're not arguing as to who's turn it is to do the dishes or walk the dog. All their petty quarrels and differences have magically disappeared for now, as they come to be by the river on a balmy, summer evening. Stealing kisses in the shadow of the tower as she casts her spell over them in what is arguably one of the most romantic places in Paris."

Jason sat there with his eyebrows slightly raised, and I could almost see his brain whirling away as he tried to take in what I was saying.

"Then, in the evening, she is all lit up in golden lights. It is almost as though she has come, perhaps in all her finery, to meet a lover at a predetermined, secret, late-night rendezvous down by the river, which is perhaps not quite so secret anymore. Nevertheless, she stands there waiting patiently in all her golden splendor. Then, every hour on the hour, she puts on a dazzling display of sparkling lights to the delight of all who can see her. While all the while, her searchlight atop the tower scans the horizon in all directions, looking in vain for some sign of her approaching lover, who never appears. Sadly, as the evening hours pass, she eventually fades alone, once again, into the darkness of the night. Only to reappear again tomorrow, full of the love and loyalty she radiates out across Paris, ever hopeful that maybe tonight, he will come."

We sat there for a moment in silence, before I let out a composing sigh and signaled to George that we needed the bill.

"Wow!" said Jason, breaking the silence.

"Yeah. She makes me think and reminds me that things are not always what they seem on the outside. Like people, no matter what defense mechanisms they have developed nor the face they show to the world, you never know what struggles or heartache may be lurking just below the surface. I guess that's why I miss her the most."

"I honestly never thought about anything remotely like that before."

"Maybe that's because you have your face stuck in your phone too much" I sniggered. "Do yourself a favor, lift your head occasionally and take in all the beauty of the real world around you."

Jason just sat there, scoffed and rolled his eyes.

"Anyway, we better be getting back. I need to go out and run some errands this afternoon."

CHAPTER 17

After speaking briefly with George, to have him add our breakfast to my account, we headed homeward along the beach.

"So, what was your favorite restaurant in Paris?" asked Jason.

"Oh, that's a tough one. There were so many to choose from, but I do have a few favorites, depending on where I am and what sort of mood, I am in."

"Such as?"

"Well, one of them is a place you may be familiar with yourself. It's called Le Bouquet des Archives in Rue des Archives in Le Marais."

"Hmmm…not sure I know it."

"Oh, it is a great place. It is all painted yellow with green awnings and large bi-fold doors that open out onto the street in summer. You could sit out there and have a cheeseboard and a carafe of wine and watch, what at times felt like all of Paris, walking by. For me, you really couldn't get a more typically French experience if you tried. The food was always very good and inexpensive. The atmosphere, being a gay friendly type of place which attracted a reasonably gay patronage, was always so nice and comfortable. The best part though was the staff. I became a bit of a regular and they would always treat me so well, almost like I was part of the family. Sometimes I would go there with friends but often I would go alone. Having such a warm friendly welcome really made me feel at home, which is an important, and often underestimated, thing when you are alone in a foreign country, and not too good with the language."

"How is your French these days?"

"Still crap and probably worse than ever because I hardly get to use it living here. However, I think I am still fluent in food and drink so at least I know I won't starve in Paris!" I chuckled.

Momentarily, my mind flashes back to that wonderful bistro and the lovely times I had there.

"I really did enjoy going there on my own, especially when the weather was good. They have those typical round bistro tables and wicker chairs that are arranged to face outwards to the street. Changes to Paris's traffic rules meant there were very few cars passing by. Just the odd bus and taxi. I remember the big leafy green tree across the street and how the dappled sunlight would filter through its leaves. I loved to just sit and watch the people, see what they are wearing, try to read the expressions on their faces and wonder what they might be thinking or where they might be heading as they strode on by. Then there were the zombies on their phones, oblivious to the fact that they nearly got run down by some maniac on one of Paris's many rental bikes as they blindly crossed the street. Of course, there were always people out walking their poochies, some of whom would stop for a scratch behind their ears whenever I clicked my tongue. The dogs, that is, not their owners!"

"I did wonder for a second," chuckled Jason

"Then late afternoon and early into the evening the crowd would change. The afternoon shoppers would disappear to be replaced by those heading home from work, if it was a weekday, and being in Le Marais, you would get all the gay guys heading out to the various bars and cafes further down the street. It was always fun to cruise the guys and see how many would make eye contact as you rated them on a scale of one to ten."

"Really, I can't imagine you doing that!" said Jason incredulously.

"I may look old to your young eyes, but I ain't dead!"

"I never really get the chance to do that. I am usually always with people and in too much of a conversation to notice."

"Yeah, or on your phone too, I bet!"

"Hmm…maybe!"

"It is one of the benefits of going out alone. Even these days, there still seems to be a stigma attached to it. You really don't see that many people out and about on their own. Sometimes I see people look at me, especially as I am older, and I can feel them thinking I must be sad and lonely, if they even bother to notice me at all that is. However, it really doesn't need to be like that. Being alone allows you to fully take in all that is going on around you in the present moment. To see things and feel things you might otherwise miss if you were having to pay attention to other people. I am not saying I want to be alone all the time, of course not, I love going out with my friends, but being alone can be just as rewarding"

"Hmm…I never really thought about it like that before."

"Maybe next time you're at a loose end, perhaps you should try it. You might be pleasantly surprised."

"Hmmm," mused Jason. "You said there were two restaurants you liked, where's the other one?"

"Oh, this one you must know. It's not far from the apartment in Saint Germain des Pres and is called Le Bosquet Saint Benoit on Rue Saint Benoit."

"No…I don't think so."

"Seriously?! You must try it out. It's a tiny little old-style bistro. It only seats about 12 people downstairs and maybe 20 or so upstairs. During the summer the front of the restaurant opens out for terrace seating, which helps expand things a bit but otherwise it is just this cozy little place hidden in Saint Germain des Pres. It serves typical French bistro food, which is always excellent and not expensive considering where it is located. The staff are also super friendly, and they treat me like one of the family whenever I go there too. It is decorated in that rustic, matt brown stain and, judging by the worn staircase leading upstairs with its gnarled balustrades and grooved stair treads, the place hasn't been decorated for a very long time. One wall is lined with mirrors, I guess to make the place seem bigger, and the rest of the walls are decorated with all sorts of tin-stamped plaques portraying French slogans and jokes as well as other more rustic paraphernalia. The tables are covered with red and white checkered tablecloths, and they often have soft jazz music playing in the background, which just makes the whole atmosphere of the place really warm and special for me."

"Hmm! Perhaps I'll give it a try when I get back to Paris."

As we arrived back at the house, we climbed the stairs up to the pool area and quickly washed the sand off our feet in the outdoor shower.

"Right, I have to pop out now and do a few things, but you'll be fine here for a while, right?"

"Oh yeah, sure."

"You know where everything is and if you get lonely, I am sure you can always chat with Mara and Paulo."

I'll be fine. I might just sleep by the pool for a while and catch some sun."

With that, I headed back to the master suite where I quickly showered, changed and headed off to town.

CHAPTER 18

Jason headed off to his room to change before going to the gym for a workout. Not having done much except eat since he arrived, he thought now would be a good time to burn off some of those extra Mara calories.

After he was done, he returned to his room, showered and, donning his speedos, made his way to the pool, fully intending to laze in the sun. Having coated himself with tanning oil he looked every inch the Greek God, with his freshly pumped, slicked up muscles on display for all to see.

As he lay there working on his tan, his mind kept going back to the events of that morning when he had managed to track down his uncle whom, he was sure, had a tear or two in his eyes. He couldn't help but wonder what was behind it and who it was that his uncle wouldn't talk about.

Eventually those nagging thoughts got too much for him. So, he decided to head into the kitchen for something to drink, hoping he might find Mara there too.

"Hi Jason," Mara greeted him as he walked in. "Can I get you something? Some lunch perhaps?"

"No thanks. I might just grab something cold to drink from the fridge, if that's ok?"

"Sure, go ahead, help yourself."

Mara watched Jason in silence as he stood there, perusing the contents of the refrigerator without really seeing what was on offer. Eventually, he simply grabbed a bottle of coke, closed the door and meandered towards the kitchen counter where Mara was preparing dinner.

"I know that look," Mara finally said. "I have seen that look so many times on your uncle's face."

"Huh?" said Jason as though his mind was somewhere else, and Mara's voice had suddenly brought him back.

"Got something on your mind?"

"Yeah, I guess."

"Come on then, out with it."

"It's uncle Charlie. Has he always talked in strange metaphors?"

"How do you mean?"

"Well, this morning we were talking about Paris, and he was going on about the Eiffel Tower like it was some sort of woman."

"Ah that! Well, you know your uncle's a very romantic man with a vivid imagination."

"Yeah, I'll say!" chuckled Jason.

"He does a lot of meditation, claims he's sensitive to people's energies, aligned with Spirit, and so on. He wears his heart on his sleeve and has never been shy in speaking about his feelings…unlike some men I know," said Mara as she rolled her eyes.

"Hmmm," mused Jason.

"I think he sees the world differently to most people too," pondered Mara

"Yeah, I guess so."

"But you have always known this, so why is this suddenly bothering you now?"

"Well, I guess that's not really what's bothering me."

"Ok, so what is?" asked Mara.

Jason let out a bit of a sigh before he continued. "Well, I went out this morning and found him pretty much where you said he would be. However, when I approached him, it seemed he had no idea I was there. It was as if he was off somewhere else, almost like he was in a trance or something."

"Well, like I said, he does a lot of meditation. So…?"

"Yeah, but that's not all. I stood and watched for a moment before placing my hand on his shoulder, which seemed to bring him back from wherever he was, and I swear there were tears in his eyes. I think he was lost in another time, thinking about somebody else."

"Ahh, ok!"

There was a pause as Jason looked expectantly at Mara, "Ahh, ok… what?"

Mara looked at Jason, "Well, it's not really me you should be talking to. This is something you need to speak to your uncle about."

"That's just it. I did ask him, but he just dismissed it. Said it was no one, 'just a shooting star'," mimicked Jason.

"Yeah, that sounds about right" said, Mara as she let out a little sigh. "He rarely talks about it."

"Then you do know what I am talking about, don't you?!"

"Well, I don't really know all that much. Like I said, he rarely talks about it."

"Well, what do you know?"

Mara stood there, as she silently scanned the look on Jason's face, all the while debating with herself as to whether she should say something or not.

"Ok," she finally said. "But you must promise me you won't tell your uncle that I said anything."

"Ok, ok. I promise."

Mara let out a much bigger sigh and motioned for Jason to take a seat as she rounded the breakfast bar. "Here, sit down," she said.

Once Jason had settled onto the barstool Mara began.

"His name, I believe, was Fabri."

"You believe?"

"Yes. This all happened when your uncle was living in Paris, long before he bought this place."

"So, who was this, Fabri?"

"I'm not entirely sure," said Mara as she dodged the question. "All I know is Fabri, according to your uncle, was the love of his life and your uncle was heartbroken when things ended."

There was a brief pause as Jason sat there, expecting Mara to say more.

"That's it?!" Exclaimed Jason. "It was just another breakup?!"

"Well, I am sure there was a lot more to it than that, but basically yes, that's it."

"Hmm…he told me about the breakup with Francisco, which sounded pretty bad, but are you saying breaking up with this…this… Fabri guy…was worse?"

"Ah huh," confirmed Mara. "Let me ask you something Jason, how many relationships have you had?"

"I don't know…a few I guess."

"And how many of them ended when you didn't want them to?"

"Ummm…maybe one or two"

"And were you heartbroken at all?"

"Sure. It's why I came here, to get away for a bit."

"Ok, so, you've had a few breakups but only one or two really hurt. Is that right?"

"Yeah, I guess so."

"And would I be right in assuming you had stronger feelings for those two, than the others?"

"Yeah," agreed Jason.

"So, clearly there are all kinds of breakups. The degree of heartache associated with each one varies with the length of the relationship, and the depth of feelings you develop during that time and so on. Some are easy to get over and a couple of weeks later you are out looking for someone new. Others can take much longer to get over and maybe, sometimes, we never do."

"So, are you saying this Fabri person simply broke uncle Charlie's heart and he's never gotten over it?"

"Well, as I said, there is probably a lot more to it than that, but yes, I don't believe your uncle has gotten over it, and I am sure he still thinks about Fabri almost every day. However, if you want to know anything more, like I said, you'll have to speak to your uncle."

With that, Mara got up from her stool and walked round to the other side of the counter and carried on preparing dinner.

"Wow! Uncle Charlie has been living here for over 5 years, and he still hasn't gotten over that guy?"

"Yep, but from what I understand, this wasn't your average run of the mill fling. It was far more intense and on a completely different level." They both sat in silence as Mara paused for a moment and then sighed. "So much so, in fact, that I am not sure Fabri just broke your uncle's heart…

…I think he burnt his soul."

CHAPTER 19

THE ERRANDS THAT I HAD TO DO TOOK A LOT LONGER THAN ANTICIPATED. Being a small island, everybody knew everyone else, and it was almost impossible to simply run an errand without bumping into someone who wanted to have a quick catch up while shopping in the menswear section of the department store, or in the freezer aisle of the supermarket.

Eventually, I made it home and had just enough time to shower and change into something a little more relaxed before joining the others for dinner. It had been a hot day, and Mara had decided that it would be a good idea to fire up the outdoor grill so we could have steaks and salad for dinner.

As I came out of my master suite, and rounded the corner to the outdoor seating area, I found Jason reclining on the sofa with one of Dr Wayne W. Dyers's books on manifestation in his hands. Mara was making final adjustments to the spread of food on the table and Paulo, as ever, was manning the outdoor grill with a cacophony of sizzling sounds and wonderous barbecue smells emanating from it.

"Ah, good. You're just in time" Mara said when she saw me. "We're all ready to go" and within barely a couple of minutes, we were seated around an array of dishes including Mara's famous orange and onion salad. There was fresh baked bread, burger buns, all kinds of ketchup and sauces, beers for the boys and the biggest platter of freshly grilled meat including steaks, sausages and burgers, that I had seen in quite some time.

"This all looks amazing, thank you guys" I said appreciatively for all the work that had gone into preparing this sumptuous banquet that was laid out before us. At that moment, I realized that I had been so busy running errands and dodging neighbors as best I could, I had forgotten to have any lunch. "I am actually quite hungry. I haven't eaten since breakfast at the Beach Club."

Apart from the clinking of beer bottles and glasses and the sound of 'cheers' as we toasted our dinner and good health, we sat in almost silence as we tucked into the various salad bowls and built our own burgers, each one of us with our own unique style. The only sounds to be heard were the gentle tapping of cutlery on plates as we sliced up tomatoes and cucumbers and the almost violent crack of iceberg lettuce as the leaves were folded and squashed into our burgers.

We continued to eat our burgers without speaking as to do both simultaneously is almost impossible. I licked my fingers and apologized for the mess on my plate of burger debris and drippings of excess sauces by passing the remark that this was clearly not 'first date' food. Then turning my attention to the more civilized faire of a big juicy steak, I asked Jason about the book he was reading.

"I see you are wading your way through 'Wishes Fulfilled' by Dr Wayne W. Dyer."

"Yeah, I found it on the bookshelf in your office. I hope you don't mind."

"Of course not! What do you think of it so far?"

"Yeah, it is kind of interesting, but I am not sure I get it. I mean do you really think it is possible to manifest things the way he describes."

"It doesn't matter what I think, Jason, what really matters is what you think. If you think such a thing is possible, decide to learn all about it and master it, you will find you can manifest anything you want…in divine timing. However, if you decide that it is all a load of woo woo hooey, then you are unlikely to manifest anything at all. If any fortunate events do come your way you will just think they are a matter of good luck, or happenstance as Dr Wayne often calls it. Which chapter are you up to in the book?"

"Umm…the one about using your imagination."

"Right. It is one of the basic principles of manifesting. Using your imagination is so very important and is something most of us either take for granted or just allow to happen in the background while our busy lives take center stage."

"Really?"

"Yes. It's really important to be consciously aware of your thoughts, so that you can use them properly to imagine the things you want and then manifest them into your reality. However, like all skills, it takes time and practice to master, which is why I try to do it as often as I can."

"Oh" said Jason who was clearly still a little lost.

"You remember me telling you what I thought about the Eiffel Tower?"

"Yes."

"Part of that was me exercising my imagination. It is why I sometimes seem to see things differently, like the Eiffel Tower, while others just see it as a metal structure." There was a pause as Jason just sat there staring at me. "Ok, I know what you are thinking and yes, many times in my life I have been called a dreamer, but I don't care."

"So, are you saying I should just sit around dreaming fanciful things like imagining buildings as people all day long? Isn't that just a bit …ummm… crazy?"

"Yep, I have been called that too, which is why I have learnt not to talk about a lot of things with people, but it is not as fanciful as you might think. Ever seen any of the Transformer films? Who do you think dreamt those up?"

"Oh, I don't count those, they are just films."

"Are they? Did the films create themselves? No. Someone somewhere used their imagination and came up with the idea of robots being able to transform themselves into cars and other metal objects, and it just grew from there."

"Hmmm…"

"But in answer to your question, no I am not suggesting you sit around all day, dreaming."

"Unlike you, you mean," chided Mara with a giggle.

"Yes, thank you. That's very funny…but no. However, what I do suggest is you take a closer look at your imagination, and how it works, because it is working every second of every minute of every day without you even realizing it."

"Really, you think so?"

"Yes, I do. So, if it is already working, does it not make sense to try to understand it and control it so that it can do the things you want it to do, rather than have it, just randomly doing things?"

"Yeah, I guess."

"So, when you think of your imagination, what is it you think of?"

"I don't know."

"Ok let's take the fanciful story of the Eiffel Tower as an example. What is that, really? Just a dream created by my imagination, perhaps?"

"Yeah, I suppose."

"Ok, so it is just a dream, but what is a dream?"

"Ummm…"

"A dream is just an organized collection of thoughts. For example: the Eiffel Tower as a woman; that she is waiting for her lover; that he never comes and she is sad; that she comes back day after day. These are all just smaller thoughts, or dreams, organized to make the larger dream. Do you follow me?"

"Yeah, I think so."

"Ok. So, the next question is how many thoughts are required before we call a dream a dream?"

"Ummm…I don't know."

"Like most things in the world, it is a spectrum that starts at one and continues up to infinity. So, going to the lower end of the spectrum, if your imagination can create a dream from a single thought just by focusing on it, then we need to be very careful as to what we think about, because, as all the books on manifestation will tell you, everything starts with a thought.

There was a brief pause as I could see Jason's brain whirling away, trying to comprehend this concept.

"Ok, but I just don't understand how it's supposed to work."

"Hmm. Well, let me see if I can explain how I understand it. Basically, I believe, it is all about energy and the frequency it vibrates at, coupled with the Law of Attraction."

"Ok, that bit I got from Dr Wayne's book, but that still doesn't explain to me how it works."

"Ok, let's start with the Law of Attraction which basically says that like attracts like. For example, if you are happy, you will attract more happiness. If you are sad, you will attract more sadness. Once you understand and accept that concept, you can then use it to your advantage by twisting things around."

"Really? How?" asked Jason.

"Simple. If you want more happiness in your life, then be happy, no matter what is going on in your world."

"So, you're saying if I just pretend to be happy, even when I am not, everything will be fine?"

"No. Pretending really isn't enough. You must feel happy to such an extent that you consciously believe you are happy. Once you achieve that, your energy will begin to vibrate at a frequency of happiness and radiate that out into the Universe where it will attract more happiness back to you. The key is getting your energy to consistently vibrate at that higher frequency."

"OK, so how do I do that?" asked Jason. "I mean everyone seems to be banging on about meditation these days, but that's really not me."

"Well, there are many ways and certainly a spiritual practice like meditation is a very powerful tool. However, if that's not your cup of tea, you could try focusing on things you are grateful for. A gratitude practice, being grateful for things, is also extremely powerful."

"Like what?" asked Jason.

"Well, anything and everything. For example: the lovely sunny day today; that you have clean water to shower with; the delicious food that Mara and Paulo so kindly prepared for us; that you had a safe flight coming here; that you live in a nice apartment in Paris; that you have a good job and the money it generates which supports the lifestyle you lead; that you have lovely friends…really, the list is endless."

"That's it?! You're saying I just have to say 'Thank You' for these things and my life will suddenly become amazing?" said Jason skeptically.

"Well, remembering to always say 'Thank You' for these things is a step forward, yes. However, if you want to make a really positive, long-lasting impact, the secret is consistency, and that's where a gratitude diary makes a big difference."

"A gratitude diary? I didn't know there was such a thing," said Jason.

"Well, you can just use a regular one. I use a one day per page diary."

"So, what do I do with it?"

"Keep it with you wherever you go and write down, every day, ten things that you are grateful for. Then write the words 'Thank You', three times after each entry."

"Can't I just do it on my phone?" asked Jason.

"Yes, you can, but I am a firm believer in handwriting a gratitude diary."

"Why?"

"Because I believe you are reinforcing the gratitude into your consciousness, and subconscious, when you are physically forming the words with your hand onto a piece of paper, as opposed to merely typing the words onto a small screen. But that's just me. The important thing is you do it however you feel most comfortable and that you do it consistently."

"And that's all I have to do?" asked Jason.

"Well, there are many things you could do, but I believe keeping a gratitude diary is a great place to start."

"Hmm" mused Jason as he finished his steak and sat back in the chair, once again stuffed with Mara's delicious cooking.

CHAPTER 20

Once we were all totally satiated with dinner, Paulo began clearing the table, while Mara went to prepare some coffee.

"So, what are some of the other things I could do?" asked Jason.

"Well, there's meditation, as we said before, which requires dedication and can take up a lot of time. Then there is being generous with your time by doing voluntary work at a hospice or animal shelter if that is your thing."

"Hmmm, yeah, I am not sure I am cut out for that sort of thing."

"Fair enough. There are other simpler things you can do such as just taking time out in nature, observing and appreciating the natural beauty all around you and being thankful for it. There are plenty of parks in Paris you could spend time in, enjoying the sun, or reading a book perhaps."

"Yeah, I guess so."

"Even something as simple as choosing different words when you speak can make a huge difference over time."

"Really?" said Jason somewhat puzzled.

"Yes, take swearing for example, those nasty little 4 letter words that people seem to throw about the place like confetti these days, can be very detrimental to your own vibrational frequency."

"Seriously? Why?" asked Jason.

"Because they convey anger, aggression and frustration and transmit negative, low vibrational energy at whomever we are directing those words at, as well as out into the Universe where it will attract more anger, aggression and frustration.

"No…surely they are just words." said Jason.

"Well, they may appear as just words that come from our mouths, but before they manifest themselves and drip from our lips like venomous poison, they first must be generated as a thought, conscious or otherwise. 99.9% of the time it is a subconscious thought."

"Really?"

"Yes, for example, when you are having a heated discussion, debate, argument or all out screaming match with someone, you don't stop and consciously think to yourself that you are going to swear at someone. You don't stand there and get all worked up, shaking with rage and say to yourself, wait…I am going to use a four-letter word. So, you muster all your strength, open your mouth and out comes, 'RATS'".

Jason burst out laughing.

"You don't then stand there and think, hmmm that didn't quite hit the mark did it. So, you try 'DAMN', but that doesn't work either. So, then you go…I know, I'll use not one but two four-letter words and that will really fix his wagon! 'HOLY CRAP!' comes out and you wait for a reaction. Meanwhile, the target of your frustration, who has been standing there looking at you like you're completely mad while you consciously concoct these things, probably just rolls their eyes as they turn and walk away."

"Yeah, I think you lost that one." laughed Jason.

"Exactly! So, in order to be able to dish out our venomous attack and get the desired effect without breaking the momentum of the discourse, we practice our swear words. We rehearse them like some military drill on a fake target and then neatly store them away in our subconscious. That way, when we are faced with the 'real enemy', we are primed and ready to strike. And that's how we end up with things that are said in the heat of the moment. With me so far?"

"Yeah, I guess so."

"Ok good. Now, the bigger issue that we don't talk about is the fact that in order to rehearse these words, we must also rehearse the emotions that go with them. We must feel the anger, the rage, the frustration so that we know instinctively how to recognize them when they appear for real so we can then trot out the relevant, venomous response. These thoughts and feelings, that we then store away in our subconscious, create negative energy and lower our vibrational frequency. As Dr Joe Dispenza is always saying, 'Where your attention goes is where your energy goes.'"

"What does that mean?" asked Jason

"Well, if your thoughts are of low frequency things, then your energy will also become low frequency. If your energy is low frequency, then you will attract more things of a low frequency because like attracts like and that is the Law of Attraction."

"But how do I know what thoughts are of a high frequency, and which ones are of a low frequency?"

"If you read books like Dr Joe Dispenza's 'Breaking The Habit Of Being Yourself', you will find charts documenting the scientifically supported fact that different emotions vibrate at different frequencies."

"Why? aren't emotions just another word for feelings?"

"No, emotions are energy in motion that causes you to react. That's why they are called emotions. It's like the energy in Einstein's Theory of $E=MC2$. E is energy, motion is movement, so e(energy) + motion(movement) = Emotion."

"Oh…I never thought of it like that before." said Jason

"So, think about it. How many times have you heard someone say, 'Oh, I read that book. It was so moving.' Or 'I was really moved by what you just said.' These people are feeling an energy in them that is being caused to move in response to some external thing or event. Or in other words, they are feeling an emotion."

"Ok, I see." said Jason.

"Good, so looking at the charts you will see all the nice things like Happiness, Joy, Love, Gratitude etc. all vibrate at much higher frequencies than the emotions of Anger, Lack, Frustration, Hate etc. So, therefore, it stands to reason that if you want more nice things in your life, you need to place your thoughts on nice things so that your energy will follow and you will attract more nice things. That is why I personally believe we should eliminate swear words from our vocabulary."

"Right, that kind of makes sense to me now, not that I swear that much anyway."

CHAPTER 21

I watched Jason as we sat there for a moment in silence while Jason thought about all we had just discussed.

"Nah...It all sounds too easy to just change my words and my thoughts and that is all I have to do, and everything will come up smelling of roses."

"Ok Jason, let me ask you this. Have you ever used the phrase, 'Gee what a coincidence, I was just thinking about you.'?"

"Yeah, sometimes, but they are just coincidences, aren't they."

"Are you sure about that? Or did you manifest a connection with that person by thinking about them?"

There was a pause as Jason was searching for something to say.

"Ok, let's try something that you may find easier to relate to. What is it you think about when you think about the kind of guys you like and want to date?"

"Oh, I don't know."

"Do you have a checklist of criteria in your mind of what you do and do not want in a guy?"

"Yeah, I guess so."

"And what do you do with that checklist? For example, if you are on Grindr and you see someone who is ok and ticks some of the favorable boxes on your checklist, do you react to his profile, or just let it sit there and see if he approaches you?"

"I guess I just kind of wait for a bit most of the time."

"And if he has characteristics on your checklist that you don't want, what do you do?"

"Oh, I immediately block him."

"Exactly, so you are doing a definite action if they are someone you don't want but you are not doing anything specific if they are someone you 'might' want, right?"

"Yeah, I suppose."

"Now think about the guys you have dated recently. Have any of them had personalities or characteristics similar to the checklist of what you do want in a guy?"

"Ummm…I don't know. They may have some of them, I guess, but most of them turn out to be guys that I don't want. Game players and so on."

"And why do you think that is?"

"Ummm…."

"Well, maybe it's because that is what you are thinking about, and instantly blocking, when you look at guys profiles. You see, when someone asks us what we want, about anything, most of the time we really don't know, right?"

"I don't know," shrugged Jason. I guess."

"Ok, let me give you an example. If I asked you, what sort of car would you have if you could have any car in the world, would you be able to give me a definitive answer straight away or would you be thinking about Aston Martins, Ferraris, Lamborghinis and so on? Or would you say something like, 'Hmmm I don't know, but I know I don't want a Skoda!' and make a bit of a joke about it."

"Yeah, definitely not a Skoda, thanks very much." Jason chuckled.

"See, a simple analogy perhaps but it kind of illustrates my point that we try to approach the question of what we do want, by giving a list of things we don't want. We are often very clear on those things, even adamant. We may call them red flags, or even deal breakers when referring to potential guys as we are so clear about them, but we are more wishy-washy about the things we do want, right?"

"Yeah, I guess so."

"So, what happens is our subconscious places more importance on the things we are adamant about, and in your case of blocking guys, even acting upon. So, those are the things that expand and end up manifesting into our reality. Hence the guys you end up dating."

"Seriously? You mean I am dating the guys I don't want because I am thinking about the type of guys I don't want?"

"Yep, that is how it works, and it is working all the time. That is why we must be very careful about what we think about. And for the record, I am just as guilty of manifesting the wrong things and the wrong guys, so don't feel too bad about it."

"Really? Like whom?" asked Jason.

There were stifled sniggers from around the table. "Ok," said Mara as she gathered up the few remaining items on the table. "Why don't you boys go and relax on the sofa."

CHAPTER 22

As we settled, once again, on the sofa in the outdoor seating area, I continued. "Yeah, for a long time, like you, I had a very firm list of guys that I didn't want in my life. A list of red flags and deal breakers such as no smokers, no long-distance relationships and not getting involved with anyone who was married or in an open relationship. I hold very strongly to my core principles of trust, loyalty, truth, openness, honesty etc. and for me, the concept of an open relationship really doesn't align with any of those."

"Yeah, but everyone is doing it these days," said Jason.

"Yes, they are, particularly in the gay world. For me though, just because everyone is doing it doesn't make it right in my mind. Any more than just because everyone is battling everyone else these days, from petty arguments to full-scale wars, doesn't make that right in my mind either."

"Wait! Hold on a sec! So, from what you were saying before about what you think about expands and having lists and red flags can cause those things to appear in your life etc., are you saying you manifested an affair with a married man?"

"Yes, I did. It was one of my absolute red flags and I was so adamant about it. I mean if I was on Grindr or some other app and I saw the guy was married or in an open relationship, I would instantly block him, the same as you would, no matter how cute he might have appeared in his photos. It was simply a deal breaker."

"So, who was he?"

"He was just a young 30 something but a truly lovely guy. He was cute, smart, funny, hardworking, sexy, fun in bed, sensible but cheeky and a bit naughty too. He was, for all intents and purposes, a good match for me."

"Don't tell me you fell in love with him!?"

"Yeah, I did. I know it was stupid, I mean he never hid the fact that he was married, right from day one and I knew exactly where I stood, again! So, it wasn't his fault, I thought I could handle it. I thought I had learnt my lesson with Francisco and could remain detached and just have some fun, but anyone who knows me knows that is never going to be the case, and this was no exception. For me, all the stars were aligned…except for one."

"Let me guess…the married star?"

"Yeah, the one I conveniently kept ignoring in the hope that it would go away or things would change, and it would line up with all the others, but I was just deluding myself…again…just like I did with Francisco."

"But is an open relationship really such a bad thing? Like I said, everyone seems to be doing it these days so what's the big deal."

"Yes, it is very common these days, particularly in the gay world as I said, and whether it is bad or not really depends on who you are. For many people it is not a problem. They're fine with it, they make it work and everyone's 'happy'. I am simply not one of those people. Perhaps I am an old fuddy duddy dinosaur, an outdated romantic if you will, but I still, to this day, believe in true love, loyalty, openness, honesty, integrity blah blah blah, and the concept of an open relationship simply flies in the face of all I stand for."

"Really?! Are you that dead against it?"

"No, not at all. I am not against anything because anything you are against weakens you, but that is another story. I am for love, loyalty and commitment. For me, in my mind, it just smacks of convenience. It's like when I want all the benefits of being married, I'll be married. However, if I go to a bar and meet some hot guy that I want to have sex with, it is now more convenient for me to be single. So, I'll wave the open relationship flag that I conveniently have in my back pocket, which conveniently absolves me from having to take any form of responsibility for my actions or the choices I make. Basically, it is just a convenient way for me to have my cake and eat it too."

"Wow! That seems pretty judgmental."

"Yeah, I know that's how it sounds but I don't mean to be. This is just how I personally feel, and I am not condemning anyone else for their actions. Each to their own, right?"

"Yeah, right."

"However, for me I could never see the logic in investing myself emotionally in someone whom, at the end of the day, will simply go home and be in the arms of someone else. However, that is exactly what I ended up doing and that is exactly what happened. I ended up being cookie jarred, and it really hurt."

"Cookie jarred? What's that?"

"I think you're all a bunch of cookies, if you ask me, and some of you are missing a few crumbs," interjected Paulo with a giggle as Mara came back from the kitchen with freshly made coffee. I just looked at him with a chuckle, rolled my eyes and turned back to Jason.

"It's called 'cookie jarring'."

"Oh, what's that exactly?"

"The term 'cookie jarring' is used to describe someone who is already pursuing a relationship with someone else but holds you in reserve, in their 'cookie jar' just in case things don't work out with the other person."

"Ah, ok."

"It often stems from the fear that the person doing the 'cookie jarring' will end up being alone if the primary relationship fails for whatever reason."

"But isn't that just…like…playing the field or something?"

"Well kind of and that isn't necessarily a bad thing, but it can become a problem if the person in the cookie jar is being made to feel like they're the only one in the 'relationship', when they're not."

"Oh…I think one of my friends was doing something like that."

"Yeah, I am not surprised because it is becoming more common."

"So, you were 'cookie jarred' by the married guy?"

"Yes. I am not convinced that he was doing it deliberately or even consciously, but that is what happened."

"What was it like?"

"It was like he was a 12-year-old boy who had caught a bug and stuffed it in a jar which he kept on a shelf in his bedroom. Several times throughout the day, he'd come and shake the jar to see if I was still alive. In my case this took the shape of sending text messages such as 'I'm thinking of you', 'I am always beside you no matter what' and

'I love you so much." Then, satisfied I was still alive, he would go off and do his homework or play with his toys etc. and forget about me. Sometimes he might have a friend over, and they would build tents and play war games and do all the fun stuff that you, as the cookie, wanted to do with him but weren't permitted to. All you could do was watch from behind the glass of your confinement jar, powerless to do anything about it except, like most bugs trapped in jar, to just give up and die."

"Oh! That sounds awful."

"Yeah, it is definitely not something I would recommend to anyone. So, keep your eyes open and avoid situations like this if you can. Also watch your own actions so you are not accidentally doing the same thing to someone else."

"So how did it affect you?"

"It brought up all my insecurities and feelings of inadequacy, not being good enough basically, not to mention jealousy and horrible things like that, which I just didn't want to be feeling. So, when it all got too much, I had to end it and walk away."

"That must have hurt too."

"Oh yeah, you better believe it!"

"So, when was this?"

"It was when I was still living in Paris. It lasted a few months and ended just before I moved here. He was another one I wanted to share all this with," as I gestured towards our surroundings. "But alas it wasn't to be."

"Another one? Who else was there?"

There was a pause as I realized I had opened my mouth and said too much. Perhaps, seeing an opportunity, Jason plucked up all the courage he could muster and said, "Was the other one Fabri?"

"Goodness is that the time?!" exclaimed Mara as she leapt to her feet. "Early start tomorrow so, I'll just clear these coffee things away and be heading off to bed."

"I take it you've been talking with Mara?" I said to Jason as Mara hurriedly gathered everything up and scurried away to the kitchen.

"She only told me his name. She suggested he was probably the guy you were remembering this morning on the rocks, but if I wanted to know anything else I would need to speak to you.

"Yeah, well Mara is right. It is late and it is too long a story and besides…it really isn't something I like to discuss anymore."

"Why not?"

"Two reasons, firstly because most people don't believe me when I try to explain what it was like, and secondly because I don't want to focus too much of my attention on him and manifest him back into my life. So, as it is late, I am going to call it a day and head to bed"

With a sigh, Jason reluctantly agreed and so we said good night and headed off to our respective rooms.

Once in the private living area of my master suite, I slumped down on the sofa. As I sat there with my eyes closed, I could see Fabri's face appearing in my mind as clearly as if he were standing right in front of me. I could feel the tears starting to well up in my eyes as I sat there remembering the contours of his face, his incredible smile, wondering if he was ok, and hoping he was happy, wherever he was.

Feeling that pang in my heart from the wound that had never healed and the all too familiar lump that developed in my throat, I let out another sigh and wiped the tears from my eyes as I got up and headed to bed.

CHAPTER 23

I woke up the next morning after a restless night's sleep. Every time I tossed and turned, there would be Fabri, lying next to me, seemingly so real that it felt as though I could reach out and snuggle myself into his gorgeous arms and make the world go away.

Feeling the dampness on the pillow from a night full of tears, I slid across the bed and, once again, sank my weary old feet into the plush, shag pile rug. After sitting in silence for a moment, I shook my head to try to dislodge the constant barrage of images of him flashing on the inner screen of my mind. Then I let out a sigh, got up and carried on with my regular morning routine.

Eventually, now fully composed and ready to face another day, I emerged from my master suite like a butterfly emerging from its cocoon. I looked around and realized it was still early and no one else seemed to be up yet. So, I decided to head down to the beach and dry my newly formed but still slightly crumpled wings in the gentle warmth of the morning sunshine.

I made my way down to the beach and into the shallows of the rippling ocean tide. I let out an audible gasp as I stepped into the somewhat cooler than expected water, venturing only as far as the depth of my ankles. It's amazing how much clarity comes from standing still and watching my feet sink into the sand beneath the beautiful clear water, feeling every grain as the tide erodes it from under my feet and deposits it between my toes, slowly burying them with each receding lap of the waves.

Looking out to sea, the gentle caress of the water around my ankles was hypnotic and I soon lost all sense of both time and my surroundings.

Suddenly, I was aware of a gentle splashing and the sound of 'oh crap!' as Jason stepped into the shallows beside me.

"Morning," I said as I snapped back to the present moment.

"Morning. I heard the gate closing as you left and so I thought I would come and join you if that's ok."

"Sure, no problem. Sorry, I didn't realize you were already up."

"It's ok. I think I am still a little jetlagged and have been waking up really early."

"Ah ok."

"So, the water is kind of…ummm…refreshing."

"I think 'bloody cold' is the expression you are looking for."

"Yeah, you're right…bloody cold! I guess it's not so bad once you get used to it, right?"

"You don't get used to it. That's just your feet going numb."

There was another pregnant pause. We appeared to have a lot of these lately. "Ok, Jason. Enough of the inane chit chat. What's on your mind?"

"I'm sorry, but I really want to hear about Fabri."

I said nothing for a moment as I stood motionless, staring out at the ocean. "You're really not going to let this go, are you?"

"He seems to have had such an impact on you, I'd really like to know about him, if that's ok."

I let the moment pass again with another pause as I continued to look out at the ocean. Then with a sigh of resignation, I gave in.

"It was more than an impact…he metaphorically opened so many doors for me. He taught me things…he showed me things…and left no doubt in my mind as to what was real beyond the 3D world of my senses. He was the catalyst for everything I learnt about manifestation and co-creating my life…it was through him that I became so closely aligned with Spirit."

"Huh?" said Jason. But I just ignored him as I continued to stand there, staring out at the ocean for what seemed like the longest time.

"He made me who I am today…he made me whole…because he was the missing piece of my soul."

I paused for a moment as I felt a tear, having broken free, creep its way down my cheek, before plunging from my chin into the cool waters of the ocean. Eventually I turned to Jason and said, "Come on, my feet are numb. Let's go and see if we can warm them up with a hot coffee."

With that we turned and splashed our way, in silence, back onto dry sand and headed back to the house. We washed the sand off our feet in the outdoor shower. The warm water did wonders to restore some sense of feeling in my toes. I made us some coffee, and we returned to the comfort of the outdoor seating area where we flopped down into the mass of cushions once more.

"So, what do you mean when you said Fabri was the missing piece of your soul?"

"He was like no one else I have ever met in my life. On the outside he was nothing out of the ordinary really, an Italian flight attendant from Naples based in the US, who liked to party hard and enjoyed meeting up whenever he was in Paris. However, there was something about him that was hard to describe. There were times when I almost felt like he was my teacher. Not in the traditional sense of the word. He didn't sit there and lecture me or shower me with pearls of wisdom or anything like that, but things that happened, the offhand things he said, had an incredibly profound impact. As a result, as I took it all onboard and reflected on things after he was gone, I learnt so much about life, relationships, myself, boundaries, expectations, you name it. It all came from him, or at least through him."

"What do you mean by that? Through him?"

"It's really hard to explain and this is where it sounds almost unbelievable to most people, but I believe Fabri and I had a very intense spiritual connection. It was almost like we were connected in some other dimension or parallel reality or something, and I think he was more of a divine channel for me than anything else."

"You're not serious?"

"Yes, I am. I tried to talk to him about it once and all he did was call me a witch and dismiss it."

"Yeah…no kidding!" said Jason with a slight roll of his eyes.

"Yes, I know it sounds crazy and why so many people didn't understand or believe me but just bear with me if you really want to hear about him."

"Ok."

There is an old proverb that says, 'When the student is ready, the teacher appears' and that is exactly what happened. He appeared."

"Just like that? What, like some kind of genie in a lamp come to grant you three wishes or something?" chortled Jason

"No, not exactly. We're not talking Aladdin or anything like that. However, evidently the time was right for me, as the student, so he started to draw me into his circle."

"Huh?"

"Don't worry it will get clearer. Just think of ever decreasing circles as I tell you how it happened."

"Ok, keep going."

"By the way, you are not alone in your skepticism. I know it also made no sense to most people, and they would often change the subject of conversation before I could fully explain things. I am sure, after a while, my friends started to think I was actually going mad. So that's why I stopped talking about him."

"But surely you must still think about him, I mean you can't simply forget someone who had such a significant effect on you, can you?"

"No, you can't and yes, I do still think about him regularly, but only in so far as hoping he is well, and happy, wherever he is. Everything else I have done my best to bury, and do not think about, because once he was gone, I didn't want to manifest him back into my life."

"Do you really think that might happen?"

"Who knows, but as all the books will tell you, what you put your attention on expands into your reality, and I became quite good at manifesting things. Hence all the books in my office."

"You mean the Dr Wayne W. Dyer books?"

"Yes, among others. Just look around you…all you see is the result of me manifesting something. I was a small-time IT person working part-time. There is no way I could afford to live in a place like this and have an apartment in Paris, unless I had manifested a windfall or two."

"Hmmm…yeah, I suppose you're right," said Jason looking around at my splendid Caribbean beachfront villa. "Ok, so getting back to Fabri, how did the two of you meet?"

"It was truly bizarre right from the beginning, so just keep an open mind, ok?"

"Ok"

"I was living in Porto and like a distant relative who had outstayed their welcome, things were getting more and more unpleasant. The apartment I had purchased turned out to be a lemon!"

"How so?"

"It was a lovely ground floor apartment which was fine in the summer but then flooded in the winter every time it rained."

"Oh"

"Yeah, so that was getting me down. Then, since Francisco had departed, I tried hard to find that magic again by dating guy after guy after guy with each one being progressively worse than his predecessor."

"Really, in what way?"

"They were users and abusers, basically. I don't mean physically abusive, but emotionally. They were like Vultures picking at the emotional carcass left in the wake of Francisco's departure."

"Yikes!"

"With each successive guy, my self-worth would take a battering, and my self-esteem slowly caved in. Over the course of a couple of years my identity ended up being completely buried, and who I truly was, was suffocated like the proverbial canary in a coal mine."

"Wow!"

"Looking back, I was a mess, a complete wreck. Yet I didn't realize it at the time. I just thought that things weren't going my way and that maybe it was time to pack up from Porto and go somewhere else and try to start a new life."

"So that's when you decided to move to Paris?"

"Actually, no. I had been in Nice in the South of France with my friend Mel, the one who is coming to stay shortly. I found Nice to be a nice small city, the climate was good, and generally I liked the feel of the place. So, I decided that was where I was going to move to. I had even started researching the cost of properties and different areas etc. That was the second of the decreasing circles, me moving to France. The first circle was him regularly coming to Europe and entering the same European circle I was in, though I didn't know it at the time."

Just then Mara appeared. "My, you boys are up early this morning. If you're hungry, I have laid out some breakfast in the kitchen, and I am making blueberry pancakes with maple syrup if anyone's interested?"

Jason and I stared at each other and in unison cried, "Hell yeah!" and with that we got up and followed Mara, and the heavenly aroma of pancakes, into the kitchen.

CHAPTER 24

After a very satisfying breakfast, as always, Jason and I stumbled back to the outdoor seating area. "I'm going to die of a heart attack if I keep eating breakfasts like that," said Jason as we slumped down into the cushions.

"Yeah, but at least you'd die with a belly full of pancakes and maple syrup dribbling from the smile on your face. There are far worse ways to go."

"Yeah, I guess you're right."

"So where were we?"

"You were planning on going to Nice but somehow you ended up in Paris?"

"Ah yes. It was late February, and I had been speaking with a friend who had moved to Paris from London the previous September. He knew the ups and downs of my life at the time, as did most of my friends. I am normally very open you know?!"

"Yes, I know!" said Jason as he rolled his eyes.

"So, he had recently moved into his new apartment and suggested I come and stay for the weekend. I checked the flights, and they were horrendously expensive. 650€ just for a return flight from Porto."

"Yikes, that's about the same as I paid to come here from Paris."

"To be fair I was looking at a last-minute flight, and they are often a lot more expensive, but there was no way I was going to pay that much just for a short flight and a weekend away. So, I started looking at alternative dates and found it was cheaper to fly up on the Wednesday with a cost of only 165€. However, I didn't want to impose on my friend during the week as I knew he had to work."

"Surely for almost 400€ you should have been able to find somewhere else to stay for a couple of nights?"

"That's what I thought. So, I got on the internet and eventually found someone who would let me sleep on his sofa bed for 45€ per night. So, I went for it."

"255€ for flights and accommodation for a long weekend is much better."

"Exactly. So, a few days later, late on Wednesday afternoon, I arrived in Paris for the first time in, probably, decades. I was staying with a guy, who was very sweet, and we spent that first evening talking. He asked me what I was intending to do while I was in Paris, to which I simply shrugged my shoulders and said, 'I dunno. Maybe I'll go to Sacre Coeur tomorrow. That seems like a good place to start, and I haven't been there for almost 35 years.'"

"Crap…I haven't been alive that long!" exclaimed Jason. "You really are old, aren't you?!"

"Shut up!!! Anyway, he suggested going to the Romantic Life museum near Pigale because it was nearby and free on Thursdays. So, with nothing better to do, that was what I did."

"Fair enough."

"Afterwards, with no real agenda or even any idea of where I was or where I was going, I found myself walking down the back streets of the 9th arrondissement in the direction of the river. All around me were these beautiful looking boucheries, boulangeries, patisseries, and any other eries you can think of. Among these were various cafes and bistros, with their tables and chairs out on the sidewalks, and waiters scurrying back and forth in their black waist coats and white aprons. It was surreal, and it all looked so magical, like I had just stepped into a movie set."

"Wow."

"It was around 5:00pm on a Thursday afternoon in February so, it was already dark, it was cold and a little damp. It was the end of the day, and as people were heading home from work, they seemed to be diving in and out of these little shops, buying things for dinner. Then, I would see a few friends sitting in a bistro laughing over a pint or two. Of course this was Paris, so there were lovers in yet another bistro, holding hands and whispering lovingly to each other over a glass of wine. Some people were just sitting having a quiet, after-work drink to wind down after a day at the office. However, it really didn't matter what people were doing. Everywhere I looked, as I strolled along, they all seemed so frigging happy!"

"Wait a sec. The French…happy? Are you serious??!!"

"Yeah, that's what I saw. I also noticed I could feel this amazing energy coming from the streets as I walked along. An energy I hadn't felt for a very long time, and looking back was something that perhaps I had been unconsciously looking for. It was at that moment that I decided, forget Nice, I need to be here, in Paris!"

"Really? Just like that?"

"Yes. Just like that. Decreasing circle number 3, moving to Paris. So, I went back to my host that evening and announced I had decided to move to Paris. 'Just like that?', he said. Yes, just like that." I chortled.

"Was that not a bit of a rash decision?"

"Yep, that's what my friend said when I announced it to him the next day. However, determined that this was the right decision for me, I spent the rest of the weekend thinking about how I would make this come about. I really had no idea, but I just knew it was what I needed to do."

Just then Paulo emerged, "I don't mean to interrupt, but the gardeners are here to tidy the garden and clean the pool, just so you know."

"Ok, no problem," I said. "I think I need to go and work off a few breakfast calories in the gym anyway."

"Yeah, me too," said Jason.

With that we headed to our separate rooms to change and rendezvoused a few minutes later in the gym.

CHAPTER 25

ONCE IN THE GYM, I FIRED UP THE STEAM ROOM AND THEN, WHEN JASON arrived, we hopped on the treadmills. Setting a brisk walking pace, we began to exercise.

"So, what happened next?" asked Jason as we settled into a breathing rhythm.

"Well, I went back to Porto and started thinking about all the pros and cons of the move. Thinking about all the things I needed to do and resolve. All the questions that needed to be answered, such as where to live in Paris, how do I rent an apartment there, what do I do with my apartment in Porto. Do I keep it as an investment and rent it out or do I bite the bullet and sell up."

"That is starting to sound like a bit of an upheaval."

"Yeah, for sure. The more I thought about it the more daunting it seemed to become, and soon I felt overwhelmed by the enormity of what I was proposing. So much so that I started to doubt and second guess myself. I started wondering if it was just a holiday thing, you know the euphoria of being somewhere new and the excitement that comes with that. I began to think maybe all my friends were right, that I was being rash, stupid and impulsive and kind of shooting myself in the foot, blah blah blah."

"So, what did you do?"

"The only sensible thing I could think of. After a couple of weeks back in Porto going over everything, I contacted the same guy who hosted me for the first couple of days and said, 'I want to come back to Paris for 5 days, is there any chance I can come and stay again?' Of course, being the sweet guy he was, he said yes. So, at the end of March, one month after my first trip, I found myself back in Paris."

"And what happened?"

"The minute I arrived I felt that energy again. I spent the next 5 days going to different arrondissements to see what felt right and where I might like to live. I talked at length with my host about the pros and cons of living in central Paris as opposed to living in the outer regions of Ile de France, like he did. We concluded that it probably would be best for me to be in central Paris, and I kind of liked the 18th arrondissement, so that was where I was going to concentrate my search for an apartment."

"So, your initial feeling about the energy was right after all and that's why you came to Paris?"

"Almost. While I was wandering around Paris during those 5 days, I felt that energy everywhere I went. In backstreet residential areas that were devoid of bistros and cafes, in parks, on the metro and even in the cemeteries. It seemed to follow me everywhere I went. Then one day it dawned on me. The energy wasn't coming from the streets of the city, but it was a person that I was suddenly convinced I would meet there in Paris, and that was the reason why I knew I had to be there."

"Seriously?"

"Yes. Anyway, enough of the treadmill. Let's do something else."

I left the treadmill and went to the mats to do some stretching and Jason moved to the weights section right next to the mats.

"So, what happened next?" asked Jason as he started doing some chest presses.

"I went back to Porto and started looking for an apartment online. By early April, I had found an apartment in the 18th near Guy Moquet station. It promised to be an excellent apartment, and I was very grateful to the agent who made the whole process relatively easy. They were all ready to sign me up and everything, but I told them I wanted to see the apartment first…in the flesh…before I signed anything."

"Well dah! Of course!"

"As it happened, I received a call from my Paris host, who by now was more of a friend, asking if I wanted to apartment sit for him for 3 weeks while he went on vacation at the end of April. Naturally I leapt at the chance and told the agent I would see the apartment then."

"Blimey, that was lucky."

"Yeah, that's what I thought too, but as you will soon see, it was just another synchronicity in the great chain of events that were drawing me closer into his circle."

"Oh? Really?"

"Yeah. Anyway, the time came for me to return to Paris. My third visit in 3 months. I spent a couple of days in Marseille, and didn't really like it very much, but that's another story. I then got the train to Paris and as soon as I arrived, there was that energy again. I contacted the agent to arrange a time to view the apartment that afternoon. When I got there, I discovered the apartment was being renovated because there was a water leak and everything had to be redecorated, which would take a few weeks. Other than that, the apartment was perfect, and I was very happy. As instructed, I sent an email confirming my intention to rent it, and all was agreed. I just had to wait for the date when it would be ready, and I could move in."

"Just like that?"

"Yep, just like that. Decreasing circle number 4 done…and speaking of done, so am I. Time for a steam."

With that I headed to the showers and the steam room, leaving Jason to finish his sets and reps.

After a short while, Jason joined me. I think the unfolding story was too much for him to concentrate on his exercise regime.

"So, when did you actually move in?" asked Jason as he sat down.

"I didn't."

"What? Why not? I thought it was all arranged?"

"Yep, so did I, but it wasn't to be, and this is where it starts to get even more weird. With the apartment all agreed I had 3 weeks to explore Paris and have fun, so I joined a Meetup group. The first event I went to was Sunday brunch held at a café in the 13th arrondissement. I was extremely shy and nervous and even though there were only 5 of us, I almost chickened out and ran away. However, in the end, I steeled myself and went. One of the guys there was a French guy, not surprisingly, who was very quiet. As my French was non-existent, everyone was speaking to me in English, but he barely said anything, so I assumed he only spoke French and thought nothing more of it."

"Yeah, that sounds familiar," said Jason

"The following weekend there was another event at the Musee D'Orsay, which I had always wanted to go to but had never had the opportunity, so I signed up and went. After the visit, which was amazing, I spoke to the organizer outside. I thanked him for allowing me to be there but apologized for not being able to stay for lunch, as I had some things to do before flying back to Porto the next day. He asked how my apartment hunting was going, so, I told him the situation. As far as I was concerned it was all sorted and I was just waiting for a date to move in. However, the reason he was asking was because the same French guy from the previous week, who had hardly said boo to a goose, was standing there and had an apartment to rent."

"No way! So, what did you do?"

"I thanked him, anyway, but explained again that I already had an apartment arranged. However, the organizer insisted I take this guy's card, 'Just in Case'. So, even though I didn't need it, I took his card just to be gracious and polite."

"Fair enough. I would probably have done the same thing too."

"I returned to Porto the next day, Monday, only to receive an email first thing Tuesday morning explaining that the apartment I was trying to rent was suffering from flooding which was coming from the adjacent building. They said it would take at least 6 months to resolve it, and they wouldn't be able to rent it to me during that time. Therefore, my reservation was cancelled, they were terribly sorry, thanks and goodbye!"

"You're kidding me! So much for decreasing circle number 4."

"No, I am not kidding you, and this was less than 2 days after being almost forced to take that guy's card."

"Ok, that is a bit weird."

"So, I had little choice but to begin my search again, which included trying to contact the French guy, unsuccessfully. So much for having his card, I thought."

"Well, yeah! That seems like it was a complete waste of time."

"Yeah! That's what I thought. However, right now I am getting hungry and I am starting to wrinkle, and I don't need any more of those at my age. What do we say we head back upstairs and see if we can grab a sandwich or something. I think the gardeners have probably gone by now."

"Yeah, sounds fine to me."

"Cool…meet you in the kitchen."

With that we shut everything down, left the gym and headed to our respective rooms to shower and change…once again!

CHAPTER 26

When I returned to the kitchen, I found Jason had beaten me to it and was chatting with Mara who, as always, was one step ahead of us, and in the process of making delicious club sandwiches and scones for lunch.

"Ah, there you are," said Mara. "I assumed you both would have worked up an appetite in the gym, so I thought I'd make us all some lunch."

"Oh, that's wonderful, thank you." I said appreciatively. I really don't know what I would do without her and Paulo, I thought to myself.

"Ok, why don't you boys go and relax outside while I finish up in here."

"Wow," said Jason as we sat down at the outdoor dining table. "It's turned out to be another amazing afternoon. Don't you get tired of all this sunshine?"

"Yeah, sometimes. After a long spell of wall-to-wall sunshine, day in day out, you do kind of miss the rain and even start to crave it. Of course, here in the Caribbean you must be careful what you pray for, especially during hurricane season." We both chuckled a little. "Now where was I?"

"You were just starting to look for an apartment again after losing the first one."

"Ah, yes. Quite right. I started looking online from Porto but suddenly found it almost impossible to even get a response from agents, presumably because I was not currently in Paris, let alone actually securing any viewings. However, I persevered and by the second half of May I had managed to get an agent to agree to show me an apartment near Bastille on Wednesday. It was now Tuesday evening the night before, so I hastily booked a flight for first thing in the morning. By early afternoon, I was back in Paris for the 4th time in as many months, standing outside a building, waiting to view this apartment."

"Bloody hell! You just dropped everything and flew to Paris?"

"Yeah, that's the flexibility that comes from not having a boss! Anyway, the apartment was a small 1-bedroom apartment. It was on the ground floor, unfurnished, a bit run down and in need of a good scrub and a lick of paint."

"Sounds like a bit of a dump."

"Yeah, it was, and an expensive one too. However, I told the agent I was interested but wanted to just check the area before committing to anything. He duly noted my details but told me I had to confirm that day if I wanted it as he had 100 people lined up to view the apartment."

"100 people??!!"

"Yep, and sure enough, as I left the building, there was a sizeable queue forming outside. Mostly young people who looked like a bunch of film extras lining up for a casting session."

"So, were you seriously considering renting it even though it was a dump?"

"Well, yes. I mean I had put myself under a lot of pressure flying to Paris like that. I was frustrated at not being able to find anything to date and was starting to feel kind of desperate. So, yeah, I was considering it as an option."

Just then Mara emerged from the kitchen with the delicious lunch she had prepared for us, with Paulo close on her heels carrying some beers for the boys. As Mara spread lunch out on the table, Paulo handed me a beer and said "Mara tells me you're telling the story of…you know" as he kind of slightly jerked his head repeatedly to the right so as not to say Fabri's name, but instead, looked like he was having a small seizure.

"Yeah, I am"

"Good," said Paulo. "Where are you up to?"

"Just viewed the apartment in Bastille."

"Ah! Do carry on!" said Paulo giving a sage like nod as he sat down to his lunch, while raising his hand and gesturing for me to continue like he was some sort of Godfather in a Mario Puzo film.

We all chuckled as I stared at him and then rolled my eyes as Mara brought him back down to Earth with a clip around the back of his head. Mara then sat down, and we all got stuck in to eating lunch.

"So, what about the apartment? What did you do?" asked Jason.

"Well, I wandered around the neighborhood, decided it was ok, found a bistro for lunch and from there, sent an email to the agent confirming I would take the apartment."

"Wow! Just like that?" asked Jason incredulously.

"Yeah, just like that…again!"

"So that was like, what, decreasing circle 4 again?" asked Jason.

"ALAS NO!" chimed in both Paulo and Mara in unison before I could utter a word, and then, unable to contain themselves, they promptly burst out laughing.

"You're both fired!!!" I retorted, as they struggled to contain their guffaws.

"It wasn't decreasing circle 4 then either?" asked Jason a little confused.

"No, it wasn't. To this day I still have not heard back from the agent."

"Oh, what??!!"

"Yeah, well, as luck would have it, I had also managed to get hold of the French guy from the Meetup group earlier that morning and arranged to meet him for lunch on the Friday. The apartment was in the 14th arrondissement. This is an area of Paris that I did not know, is on the left bank, which I am not sure I had even ventured to yet, and was not where I was even looking to live. I was also nervous about meeting him as he didn't seem to speak English, and my French was still non-existent. However, I thought, what the hell, I would go and check it out anyway."

"What do you mean *was* non-existent. It still *is* non-existent," laughed Paulo.

"Yes, thank you! Don't you have a pool to clean or something?"

"Me? Nope! All done, said Paulo as he sat there grinning like The Cheshire Cat from Alice in Wonderland."

"So, anyway," I continued. "When I arrived, I messaged him to say I was there. He came down, opened the door, stuck out his hand and said, 'Good morning, come on in' in perfect English."

"No!!"

"Yep, and all my anxiety briefly melted away. He led me to the first floor and showed me the apartment, and not yet knowing how much the rent was, I said to myself 'there is no way I can afford this.' And my anxiety levels went shooting back up to where they had previously been. I mean the apartment was not newly decorated, but it was fully furnished and had everything I needed, was clean and comfortable, quiet and had a private terrace, which is a huge bonus in Paris. Even though it was only a studio, compared to the last place, this was a palace."

"So, what happened?"

"Well, bearing in mind that he didn't know me from Adam, after spending the afternoon with him, to my astonishment, he cut me an amazing deal on the apartment which was simply too good to refuse. No guarantor, no proof of income, no residency status, no background checks whatsoever. A small deposit and what I considered to be a very reasonable rent for the apartment was all that was required. I naturally accepted his generous offer and moved in in mid-June."

"Ok, so that was decreasing circle number 4 then, right?"

"Yes, it was. They say everything happens for a reason and I am not sure why it worked out this way, but I am eternally grateful to my new landlord for his kindness. Allowing me to rent his apartment moved me into a smaller circle. A circle I would never have encountered had I remained in the original apartment in the 18th or been accepted to rent the apartment near Bastille."

"Wow" said Jason. "That's amazing."

"Yes, so once I moved in, the stage was now set for me to meet Fabri. Of course, I didn't know it yet, but now it was just a matter of time until our paths crossed."

CHAPTER 27

"Well," said Mara. "If everyone has finished, I'll just clear these dishes away. Coffee anyone?"

"Yeah, I wouldn't mind one if that's ok?" I replied.

"Jason?" asked Mara.

"No, I'm good with a beer thanks."

"No problem. I'll bring you a cold one."

"Yeah, well I suppose I should get on as well," said Paulo. There's always lots to do. Catch you guys later." With that both Paulo and Mara got up and left the table.

Although the morning had started out somewhat fresh, the temperature had steadily climbed and now it was quite a hot afternoon. We dragged an umbrella over to the edge of the pool for some welcome shade and dangled our feet in the cool water. Jason and I sat there for a short time, just gazing into the waters of the pool without saying anything. Although the pool always looked clean, I was constantly amazed at how much more the water seemed to sparkle after the maintenance gang had been. When the gentle sea breeze rippled the surface, and the sun caught it just right, it was like looking at a million diamonds scattered across a jeweler's cloth, but try as you might, you were never quite able to fix your eye on the one that sparkled the most before it disappeared.

"So, I assume after all that, that your paths did eventually cross, right?" asked Jason, bringing me back to the present moment as Mara approached with our drinks.

"Yes. Even though I was bouncing between Paris and Porto, tying up loose ends and sorting out what I wanted to bring to Paris, and what was going to get jettisoned, it really didn't take very long at all. A few weeks maybe."

"Here you go boys" said Mara as she placed the drinks on a small table behind us. "I brought you some iced tea too. It is hot out here and you both need to make sure you are drinking enough."

"Thank you, Mara, you're a star," I said as she smiled, gently ruffled my hair, turned, and headed back towards the kitchen. I grabbed my coffee as Jason reached for his fresh beer.

"So, how did it happen?" asked Jason, getting more impatient as the day wore on. "The crossing of the paths, I mean."

"Initially he contacted me online. He had found my profile on Grindr due to my proximity to him, the result of the decreasing circles. After a while of chatting, a few delays and a little stalling on my part, due to what I perceived were quite a few 'red flags', I gave in to his determined pleading, plucked up the courage, and agreed to meet."

"He had 'red flags' but you still agreed to meet?"

"Oh yeah. He had so many 'red flags' I thought it was a carnival."

Unable to control himself, Jason let out a laugh almost choking on his beer, "And?"

"By now it was mid-September. The full heat of summer had passed, the days were getting noticeably shorter, and the morning air was much cooler requiring me to wear a jacket. We agreed to meet outside his hotel, decreasing circle number 5, which as it turned out was only 200 yards from my apartment."

"Seriously?"

"Yes. He was coming in on an early flight and expected to be at the hotel by around 7:00am. Knowing that the mornings were much cooler now, he had instructed me to go into the hotel and wait in the lobby."

"And did you?"

"Hell no! I stayed outside on the street trying to look inconspicuous, hiding among the tall pot plants that flanked the hotel entrance, like some Russian spy waiting for a clandestine rendezvous with his contact. My mind was a blaze with doubts and insecurities and the voice screaming in my head, what the hell are you doing you old fool!"

"Hahaha," chortled Jason.

"I had never done anything like this before. I mean who meets anyone for a date or even just a hookup at 7:00am in the morning? Plus, I had never even met anyone in a hotel before. What the hell am I doing. 'Go wait in the lobby,' he says, but what if someone sees me and asks me what I am doing there. How would that go?"

"Excuse me sir, are you a guest in the hotel?"
"Ummm…no, I am waiting for a guest."
"And which guest would that be, sir?"
"Ummm…Fabri"
"I see. And that would be Fabri who, sir?"
"Ummm." Panic now setting in!
"Well, what room is this Fabri person staying in, sir?"
"Ummm…I don't know, I don't think he has checked in yet."
"I see, sir!"

"Blah blah blah. So, you can see why I was standing outside in the cold. With all this churning away in my head like an old agitator washing machine, I was in no state to try and bluff my way through anything. My palms were starting to feel clammy, and my pulse was racing. I was even starting to perspire, though it was probably only around 10 degrees C outside."

"Oh my god! It sounds like you were becoming a nervous wreck!" said Jason

"Yeah, I was. Then the insecurities and self-doubts took over, and crashing into each other in my mind like dodgems at the fairground, were things like; Maybe this is all a game and I am being played with; What if this is some kind of set up?; What the hell am I going to do if he turns out to be some kind of psycho axe murder?; Oh my god what am I doing here?; Where is he?; He's not here; He's not coming; This is just a load of nonsense and I am left here looking like a fool for someone else's amusement; That's it, if he isn't here in the next couple of minutes, I am going home; This is stupid, what the hell was I thinking."

"Holy shit…that was all going on in your mind?"

"Yes, I was very quickly becoming an absolute basket case. Then, suddenly, the phone in my hand that I had been obsessively checking all the while I was standing there, shuffling from foot to foot and trying not to pee myself in terror, buzzed. It was him with a simple message, *I can see you*."

"What?" exclaimed Jason

"As I read it, I thought, oh god! He is an axe murderer and has been watching me from some vantage point like a sniper about to fire. In panic I looked around but all I saw was a coach pulling up at the hotel. So, I messaged back and asked if he was on the coach, which he confirmed he was. Somehow, now having a target to focus on, I oddly started to feel a little less panicked."

Sitting there by the pool, reliving the scene as I related it to Jason, I started to feel all the same anxiety and emotions beginning to awaken within me. The same ones that I had tried so hard to bury long ago.

"I just stood there and watched as the doors opened, and the flight crew all began to descend from the coach to collect their luggage. Being a wide boulevard with dedicated taxi ranks and hotel pick up lanes etc. the coach was a good 50 meters away from where I was standing. I looked and looked, but I could not see him at all. He was nowhere to be seen."

"Really?!"

"Yeah, there were several women in the crew and only a couple of guys that I could see. With my overthinking mind now in super turbo mode, I began to think he must have faked his photos on his profile, that maybe he was this guy or maybe that one, neither of which stirred any interest in me at all. This was all just too much for me to cope with, panic started to set the fears in my mind ablaze like a ragging forest fire, and I felt I needed to get away…now!"

"Shit! I think I might have started to run at this point."

"Just then, as some of the crew started to move away towards the hotel, a guy who had been bending over to pick up his flight crew luggage stood up, turned, and flashed me one of the biggest smiles I had seen in a very long time. That was it. I knew, in that instant, he was the one I was destined to meet here in Paris. He possessed the same energy that I had been feeling for the past 6 months, and even though he was across the wide boulevard, the wave of his energy hit me like a truck. He had a smile that could melt steel, and my jaw hit the floor. I couldn't believe it was him. That I was finally seeing the source of that energy in the flesh, and for the only time in my life that I can remember, I felt like I started to swoon.

"Swoon?! Seriously??"

"Yeah, swoon, like a 1930's Hollywood movie star with the back of her hand on her forehead, swaying as she is about to faint," I mimicked.

"So, what happened?"

"He gave a slight nod towards the hotel entrance, which I took to mean to follow him. I then watched him as he strode across the pavement in his uniform with his head up, brimming with confidence and self-assuredness. His broad shoulders were back, pulling his shirt across his well-developed chest. His gorgeous arms on display in his pure white, short sleeved shirt, the muscles flexing as he pulled his luggage along, up the curb and into the hotel. I slowly stepped into the hotel behind him, at a discreet distance of course, and followed the most amazing butt I think I had ever seen. His uniform pants perfectly cradling each cheek before flowing down over two very well-developed thighs."

"Oh!" said Jason with raised eyebrows.

"He checked in and got his room key while I loitered in the lobby trying to look relaxed, hoping to give off the illusion that I belonged there, when in fact I was nothing more than a quivering bowl of Jello. He re-emerged from the reception desk and headed towards the bank of elevators. Naturally I followed like a puppy dog, and we entered the elevator along with several other people. I stood away from him in the back corner of the elevator and clung to the railings as I was now trembling all over and I could feel the perspiration on the back of my neck soaking into the collar of my polo-shirt."

I shuffled a little at the pool's edge so that I was now sitting on my hands, as they too, were visibly shaking from the emotions now coursing through my body as I recalled the scene.

"Now that I was close enough, I discreetly stole furtive glances at him. I could see, for the first time, just how gorgeous he was and that his profile photos didn't do him any justice at all. The chiseled features of his brow, nose, cheek bones and the line of his jaw were as though they were carved from marble and covered with beautiful, slightly tanned olive skin. Occasionally he would turn and catch me glancing at him, give me a half smile and a seductive wink. I have no idea if anyone said anything in the interminably long elevator ride, but I doubt I would have heard them anyway. All I could hear was the thunderous beating of my heart in my chest, which I was convinced was going to explode any minute."

"Wow! Was he really that gorgeous?"

"Well," I sighed. "I thought so, at least he was to me." Hearing my own voice cracking a little. I turned to look at the ocean as I began to feel the pang in my heart from the wound that had never healed and the all too familiar lump developing in my throat. Jason, sensing that things were getting a bit emotional for me, said nothing. He just sat patiently in silence, though I could feel his eagerness to hear what happened next. I turned back after a few moments and continued.

"We finally got to our floor, the last ones to exit the elevator with another person who fortunately headed off in another direction. We walked along the corridor looking for his room with him saying nothing more than 'hey, how are you doing?' and me? Nodding and smiling sheepishly at him, was all I could muster."

Jason just sat there in silence while I paused again, my head slightly lowered and gazing aimlessly into the pool.

"We entered his room", I continued, my speech faltering a little, "the final decreasing circle number 6, and I stood there at the end of the bed, speechless and shaking like a leaf while he placed his luggage in the corner of the room. Then, in one sleek, swift, manly but ever so gentle movement, he came over to me…

…took my face in both of his hands…

…and kissed me like I had never been kissed before."

Feeling a tear welling up in my eye, I turned back to the ocean as I felt it break free and run down my cheek.

CHAPTER 28

Jason didn't say anything while I composed myself. He simply poured me another glass of iced tea. I was somewhat overwhelmed with emotions as though I were right back there with Fabri, it felt so real. So, I took a few deep breaths to calm the surge of emotions and anxiety that was coursing throughout my body and wiped away the tears that were gently rolling down my cheeks. When I felt sufficiently under control again, I turned back to Jason and gratefully accepted the glass of iced tea as my mouth and throat had suddenly become very dry.

"Are you ok?" asked a concerned Jason.

"Yeah, I'm fine."

"I am sorry, I didn't realize he still affected you so much."

"It's ok. It was years ago, and it's reasonable to think I'd be over it by now, but…" and I just shrugged and drank some more tea.

"You really loved him, didn't you?"

A nod of confirmation and a whispered "Yeah," was about all I could utter at this point for fear of bursting into tears.

Jason had had a few beers and quite a bit of iced tea and announced he needed to pop to the toilet. I watched as he disappeared inside the house, heading for the guest bathroom, and the moment he was out of sight, I used the opportunity to escape to the sanctuary of my master suite to compose myself properly. I crashed onto my bed, face down, buried myself in the pile of pillows and just lay there. With my eyes closed, all I could see was the image of Fabri, as clear as day, while the memory of that first kiss relentlessly assaulted my mind and brought everything that I had buried so long ago, flooding back.

I don't know how long I laid there but eventually the trembling emotions subsided. It was late afternoon, and the sun was quickly descending in the sky. The heat of the day was gone, and the temperature was now dropping too. So, I decided that a shower and a change of clothes would probably be a good idea.

Still with the same pang in my heart from the wound that has never healed, I striped off and climbed into the shower. I have one of those extra-large rain shower heads, so I adjusted the water pressure and temperature, and just stood there, letting the water cascade over me as though I was standing in a tropical rainstorm. I closed my eyes, and I was immediately back in the various hotel rooms I had shared with him, remembering all the times we showered together.

Due to the flight schedules, he only stayed for 24 hours at a time, but during that time we might shower at least 2 or 3 times together. I loved scrubbing his back. He worked out and did a lot of work on his lats, so he had the most perfect V-shaped back I had ever seen. I loved to massage his shoulders and the back of his neck right up into the base of his skull. The flood of water as it cascaded down his back made his beautiful olive skin feel as smooth as glass and my hands would simply slide over his back, like an ice skater gliding along on a single knife-edged blade, all the way down to his perfectly toned butt.

From time to time, I would kneel and wash the backs of his legs, massaging from his calf muscles all the way up to his lower back. Being on his feet so much during the flight, his leg muscles would often be very tight.

He clearly enjoyed showering with me too as sometimes, when I was done, he would turn around, gently take the sides of my head and guide my mouth onto his now fully erect and throbbing cock. It was incredible how perfectly it would fill my mouth, all the way to the back of my throat where sometimes it would make me gag a little. The water from the shower would be pouring down from his chest and smothering my face. It made it hard to breathe while I worked on him, but I didn't care because he tasted so damn good! I would glide my hands up his slightly toned stomach and, deflecting some of the water, I would search blindly for his nipples. They were sensitive and having me play with them at the same time would drive him crazy. He seemed to love what I was doing so much that it really didn't take long for me to push him beyond the point of no return, until he lost all control and would explode, shooting his large load down the back of my throat.

Once he was done and regained his composure, he would gently help me to my feet and wrap me up in his gorgeous arms. Then we would passionately kiss and kiss under the warm flooding waters of the shower, while the final remnants of his euphoria ebbed away.

Back in my own shower, I opened my eyes and brushed the water away from my face. I had no idea how long I had been there. The concept of time has a habit of becoming all distorted when I am lost in the memories of Fabri. However, I realized that, while I was standing there in the shower, tears had been running down my face and mixing with the warm water, only to be washed away down the drain forever.

Turning the shower off, I stepped out, grabbed a towel and started to dry myself down. Feeling a little drained, I concluded that I had probably cried away a lot of the pent-up emotions from the afternoon. I continued drying myself, then heaved a big sigh as I hung the towel up on the rail to dry and went to change into something more comfortable, and slightly warmer, for the evening.

Feeling somewhat more human I stepped out of my master suite just in time to see the last flickers of the sun sinking into the depths of the ocean. I rounded the corner to the outdoor seating area where I found Paulo, Mara and Jason all sitting chatting.

On seeing me Mara got to her feet, gave me a big hug and kiss and asked, "How are you feeling?"

"I'm ok, just a little drained. Perhaps I need a little something from the bar."

"What a champion idea," exclaimed Paulo. "What will you have?"

"Ummm…any chance of a Mai Tai?"

"Coming right up," said Paulo. "Anything for anyone else?"

"Yeah, a Mai Tai sounds good," said Jason while Mara opted for a glass of white wine.

Paulo headed off to the bar. He was a little heavy handed when it came to mixing cocktails and frankly a strong drink was really what I needed right now.

"I have decided to have a night off," Mara announced, "so we thought we would just order some pizzas and chill this evening."

"Sounds perfect. To be honest, I am not really that hungry."

Mara and I sat down on the sofa and Jason said, "I am really sorry to get you all worked up like that, Uncle."

"Well, that's another reason why I don't talk about Fabri much, but it's fine, don't worry about it."

Paulo soon returned and we all settled down for a drink and a chat.

"So that was how Fabri and you met," said Jason.

"Oh Jason!" reprimanded Mara as she glared at my nephew.

"Mara, it's ok," I said. "I'm feeling a little better now. Yes Jason, that was how we met."

"It just sounds so bizarre," said Jason.

"Well, that's because it was bizarre…truly bizarre. Six decreasing circles, lined up over a six-month period by a long string of seemingly random yet interconnected synchronistic events, far too numerous to simply be dismissed as mere coincidences. Six circles that took me from Europe, to France, to Paris, to the 14th arrondissement, to his hotel, to his room, where I found myself caught like a helpless fly, stuck in the very center of the spider's web he had woven."

"But it just sounds so unbelievable," said Jason. "I mean are you saying it really was fate that you met the way you did?"

"I have no idea who nor what was behind all of this. You can call it fate if you want or God, The Universe, Divine Spirit, or whatever. The fact is something orchestrated us to be together, there's no two ways about it in my mind."

"But why? I don't understand," said Jason.

"Because I was ready, and when the student is ready, the teacher appears. At that point, there was absolutely nothing that would have prevented us from meeting, and despite eventually getting my heart very badly broken, it was worth every tear, and I am eternally grateful to whatever it was that brought us together."

CHAPTER 29

"So, was it love at first sight then?" asked Jason.

"To be honest I am not sure. Certainly, in this life, I fell in love with him that night, but it also felt like I was already in love with him before we met, like we had loved each other in another time, another place."

"Seriously?"

"I know it sounds weird and something out of a corny B-Grade Hollywood movie, but that was how it felt. However, regardless of that, that first night was incredible and yes, I did fall in love with him right there and then."

"What happened?"

"The world vanished."

"What? What do you mean?"

"As soon as we arrived in the room, bearing in mind it was about 7:30am and the world was just starting to get on with its day, the first thing he did was block out any light coming in the windows. Being a 5-star hotel, the rooms were soundproofed and equipped with blackout curtains. So, the minute he shut out the light, and with no noise, there was nothing but us. We quickly undressed and showered together, set the room up so that there were no phone interruptions, we grabbed the complimentary water from the mini bar and then climbed onto the bed and into each other's arms. The lights were off, and the room was lit only by the soft glow of the hotel welcome message on the television. We talked and joked and laughed. We played with each other, had sex and made love for hours on end. Then eventually we would try to sleep, cuddled-up together."

I paused and they all sat in silence while I stared into space before continuing...wistfully.

"It was incredible every time I was with him, even from the first night, we were never awkward or uncomfortable sleeping together and we would change positions in unison as though we were one. It was as though we just melted together like hot chocolate and vanilla ice cream, and we would stay like that until morning came. Then, suddenly, as if we were returning to Earth, it was back to reality. We'd shower, get dressed, tidy the room and then I would discreetly leave before him so no one would suspect anything as he rendezvoused with the crew for his return flight."

"Wow! That sounds amazing."

"Yeah, it was incredible. It was as though the elevator had taken us up to a heavenly place, high in the clouds above the city. The minute we entered that room, time ceased to exist and there was nothing outside of that room, outside of his arms. It was as though he took me into our own tiny little universe, just for the two of us."

"How come you never say things like that to me?" jibed Mara to Paulo and poking him in the ribs with her finger. We all laughed, and Paulo just shrugged. "It's ok, he is very romantic in his own ways, and I wouldn't change a thing," said Mara as she leaned in to give Paulo a kiss.

"Get a room you two!" said Jason and we all burst out laughing again.

The laughter died down and I sat there still staring into space and reminiscing.

"You're thinking about him, aren't you?" said Jason. "I can tell by the goofy look on your face!" he chortled.

"Well, yeah guilty as charged. I was just remembering that even though he was gorgeous, smart, funny and sexy as can be with a stunning body, the best part for me was sleeping with him. Or in my case not sleeping with him."

"What do you mean, 'not sleeping with him'?"

"Whenever we were together, I hardly ever slept at all. I would just wrap him in my arms, or me in his, and I would just watch him as he slept. It was so amazing, I never wanted to miss a single moment by sleeping."

"You'd stay awake just to watch him sleep?" asked Jason.

"Yes, of course. You should try it some time. For me it wasn't a problem because I could always catch up on sleep the next day, after he was gone."

"Isn't that kind of…creepy?"

"It doesn't have to be, and it doesn't have to be for the whole night either, just an hour or two."

"Why?"

"Because they say when someone is sleeping, all their defenses are down. The persona they project to the world switches off and all the masks they wear fall away. That is when you get to see who that person really is."

"But how can you see who they really are. They are asleep!!!"

"Yes, they are asleep. However, if you watch closely and listen with your heart, all will be revealed."

"And I suppose that was what you did with Fabri, right?"

"Yep! Right from that very first night when I saw, for the first time, the full power of his heart. It was enormous and it radiated such intense light and energy that it was like a galaxy of a million stars. The same stars that sparkled in his eyes and radiated out through his smile."

"Seriously?"

"Yes, and the more time I spent with him the more I came to realize he was a beacon. People were naturally drawn to his very masculine energy. He was a born leader and a natural motivator and could get people to do anything he wanted."

"It sounds amazing and clearly you were deeply in love with him, but was it reciprocated or was it just a fling whenever he passed through town?" asked Jason.

"It wasn't just hotel time. He invited me to stay with him for a long weekend, a few weeks after we met and it was wonderful. I got to see the real him in all his glory. He was an amazing host who wouldn't let me do anything but sit and be waited on. He showed me incredible kindness, warmth, and affection and he had boundless generosity as he paid for virtually everything the whole weekend. I was only there for three and a half days but to be able to be with him exclusively for the whole time was truly amazing. For me it was an incredible time and a wonderful memory that I will cherish forever."

I paused again as we all sat there in silence once again before I continued.

"Cudda, Shudda, Wudda!" I suddenly said. "The weekend spent with him showed me that it could have been reciprocated, and him sensually playing with the ends of my fingers under the pillow every time we cuddled and slept, supported that. There are times when I thought it should have been reciprocated and that we let a huge opportunity pass us by. Then I think to myself that it probably would have been reciprocated, if that was what he came to me for. However, I now know that it wasn't."

"Really? What did he come for?"

"Like I said before, when the student is ready, the teacher appears. He came to teach me…he came to rescue me."

CHAPTER 30

Suddenly there was a ding-dong from the front gate as the pizzas that Mara had ordered arrived. Paulo leapt to his feet to go and retrieve them, while the rest of us went to the kitchen to organize plates, napkins and drinks. Opting for a completely casual dinner we decided to simply eat around the glass-topped coffee table of the outdoor seating area. Moments later Paulo returned with 4 very large pizzas of varying flavors, spread the boxes across the coffee table and we all dived in, once again eating in silence. I used the respite to try to quell any further buried emotions that might suddenly boil their way to the surface again.

While reaching for his third slice of pizza, it was Jason who spoke first. "I think I am a little confused."

"Oh? How so?" I asked.

"Well, it all sounds amazing and perfect and idyllic etc. and maybe the kind of situation we all dream of, but how exactly did he rescue you? I mean if you were still together and life was all happiness and rainbows, then that I could understand. But here you are alone, and he is nowhere to be seen. So, I don't understand how that taught you anything?"

"That's because I chose to remember the good bits, the fond memories and feelings, the excitement of that first encounter, all the positive aspects of what we 'had'. The truth is it wasn't all beer and skittles. Fabri had, what I considered, a darker side to him, but I did my best to turn those negatives into positives too. Almost as though I was using all the bullshit as fertilizer to help me grow, if you will."

"Really?"

"Yes, between the wonderful times of showering together, sleeping with him and even staying with him at his place, there were other times he treated me really badly."

"How?"

"He would make promises and break them all the time. It got to a point where if he used the phrase 'I promise', I knew he had no intention of ever following through on whatever he was promising. It was just words he thought I wanted to hear. Breadcrumbs to keep me alive while stuck in the center of his web. He'd come up with bullshit excuses to get me out of the room, like going to get something for us to eat, to only then leave me sitting in the lobby of the hotel, literally for hours, while he entertained a chorus line of guys in his room that he managed to lure in from Grindr. Other times he would project nonsense on to me. He'd say things like 'my problem was I craved attention.' Whilst I didn't believe it was true, it did make me stop and think if there was any truth to it and I just wasn't seeing it, or refusing to see it, or whatever."

"But…" Jason paused somewhat confused. "I thought it was that pipe smoking dude that said that to you?"

"'The Pipe Man'…it was," I said.

"Wait a minute! You're telling me that this amazing sounding Fabri guy was actually 'The Pipe Man'?"

"Two sides of the same coin," I confirmed with a gentle nod.

"Why didn't you just tell him to piss off and walk away?"

"Because I was caught in his web and I didn't feel I had the strength to do so. I just kept hoping that every time he came to Paris to see me, that the toss of the coin would land Fabri face up, which it did… occasionally…but rarely."

"So, what did you do?"

"Nothing. The first flurry of us being together all happened very quickly over the course of about 8 weeks, but then after staying at his place, he seemed to vanish."

"Just like that?"

"Yeah. I felt completely rejected and it was a really tough time for me. Finances were stretched to breaking point, the weather had deteriorated in Paris as winter kicked in, and you know I don't do winters! Fabri stopped reading or responding to my texts and was effectively ghosting me. Thinking it must have run its course but without any closure, I was really upset and depressed and feeling a whole sea of emotions. Fortunately, I was able to lean on my new friends in

Paris, some of whom would contact me every day to check on me and make sure I was ok. An old friend also came to stay for a few days and helped take my mind off things. Eventually I made it through, though at times I didn't think I would, and I will always be grateful for their loyalty and support during what felt like a very dark time for me."

"You were lucky they were there for you."

"Yes, I was. Then someone recommended a couple of self-help books and so I started reading. I learnt to step back and tried to look at things including my own actions and reactions more objectively. It seemed to help too and the devasting feeling of loss began to subside, although I still loved him and missed him terribly."

Having devoured the pizzas, Mara began to clear the boxes and plates away and then headed to the kitchen to make some coffee.

"Then just before Christmas…" I continued. "I felt a sudden surge of energy again. It was Fabri, it had to be, and I was somehow convinced he was going to be in Paris for either Christmas Eve or Christmas Day, I could feel it."

"No way!"

"Yep, but of course, it didn't happen, and I was disappointed, again, and told myself that it was all in my head. However, a few days after Christmas about 3 days after I felt his energy, Fabri did in fact contact me telling me he would be in Paris for New Year's Eve."

"You gotta be kidding me! After you felt his energy, he then contacted you out of the blue, just like that?"

"Yes, and that then became a pattern that I noticed and which I journaled many times. I would feel him and usually within 3 days he would message me. The last time it happened, it was only 3 hours after I felt him, and I hadn't heard from him for almost 4 months!"

"Ok, that is weird!"

"Exactly but getting back to him coming on New Year's Eve. Naturally, though my emotions were a little confused now, I still felt over the moon at the prospect of seeing him and I met him without any hesitation. We spent New Year's Eve together and it was the most amazing New Year's Eve ever for me. I spent 9 ½ hours wrapped up with him, in his arms or with my arms wrapped around him and it was the most incredible feeling in the world."

"But didn't that just land you right back at square one?" said Jason as Mara returned with coffees for everyone.

"Yep, only now the rollercoaster of ups and downs and the swings between elation and disappointment were becoming much more pronounced. Although it was probably plainly obvious to everyone else, my feelings were so strong for him that I was confused and almost didn't know which way was up anymore. I knew it was becoming toxic and I should just walk away, like all my friends told me, but I was afraid I still didn't have the strength to escape his web. I was afraid to walk away prematurely in case things were going to improve, which was delusional, and I was afraid that I wouldn't be able to walk away without destroying my own heart, once and for all, in the process."

"That's crazy. You should have just blocked him after he disappeared!"

"Well, maybe. However, I felt I had to know once and for all if he really had feelings for me or if he was just playing games because there was always this constant 'but maybe, if only' string of thoughts eating away in the back of my mind. I felt if it was a game, I needed closure to end it. The only way I could think of knowing for sure was to somehow back him into a corner from which, if he was playing games and wanted to escape, he would have to completely reject me. In my confused state of mind, I felt that would give me the opportunity to then walk away with my heart intact. A cunning plan I thought. So, the next morning, while we were eating breakfast, I did something I never thought I would do…ever!"

"Oh god…I am afraid to ask. What?"

"I asked him to marry me!"

"You gotta be shitting me! You asked this…this…I don't even know what to call him…to marry you?!"

"Yes."

"What did he say?"

"Well, my cunning plan failed and unexpectedly, Fabri said yes without a moment's hesitation or thought. I don't know if this is truly how he felt or if he was just saying what he thought I wanted to hear, but my plan backfired. He didn't reject me but instead played with me even more, almost upping the ante."

"Sorry, I just don't get it! It now sounds like you were both playing games, trying to outsmart each other."

"Well, maybe we were because less than 2 weeks later, something very minor happened, we had a disagreement and Fabri threw me away. He told me never to message him again and he blocked me. So much for wanting to marry me."

"Ah, finally! So now the truth comes out, and he was just playing with you."

"Well, so it seemed, and I finally got the definitive rejection I was looking for even though, at the time I still felt devastated. The rest of January was again a very dark time for me though not as bad as December was. I somehow felt stronger than before. Enough to start asking myself questions like 'Why wasn't I good enough, again?' 'Why don't guys like me enough to stick around?' 'Why do I always end up feeling used and abused?' and 'What the hell is wrong with me?'"

"Yeah, I know those questions all too well."

"Then I realized, I couldn't answer those questions. I couldn't say what was wrong with 'me' because I realized I didn't know who 'me' was anymore."

CHAPTER 31

"I don't know who you are half the time, either," chimed in Paulo, "and that's just you getting up in the morning."

"Haha, yes, very funny," I said.

"Well, on that cheerful note," said Mara as she stood and started gathering up the empty coffee mugs, "I'll just clear these things away and we'll call it a day. Come on Paulo, let's leave them to it. Goodnight boys."

"Ah, that's my cue," said Paulo as he too got up to leave. "Goodnight. See you guys in the morning."

We watched Mara and Paulo head off to bed, then Jason started, "OK, so you didn't know who you were anymore. I am not quite sure I fully understand that but fine. So, what did you do?"

"Once I got over the initial shock of being blocked and rejected, and then coming to terms with the fact that it was done and I'd never see him again, I started doing a lot of work on the 'me' that I had forgotten."

"What sort of work? Like what?"

"Well, for a start I got back into doing yoga and meditation. With the upheaval of the move from Porto etc. I had let both practices slip from my daily routine. However, I felt I needed a change from the same old guided meditations that I had been doing up to that point. So, I found some others on YouTube, ones that were just sounds at various frequencies. Frequencies that are supposed to be aligned with each of the body's chakras blah blah blah."

"Oh? Did they work?" asked Jason.

I have no idea. Maybe they were simply all I needed to just clear my head for a bit as opposed to doing anything else."

"Fair enough."

Then, remembering the books I had read, I started trying to step back from everything again, and look at things from a different perspective. Being self-employed for more years than I care to remember, and now semi-retired, I couldn't remember the last time I even looked at my CV let alone updated it. So, I dug out an old one and started from there."

"Written on a stone tablet no doubt," giggled Jason.

"No, papyrus, you little shit! Anyway, it wasn't easy because I really felt so broken, but I began to review my life and the things I had achieved in the past. Sure, they may have taken place a long time ago but were, nevertheless, amazing achievements for me. Things like software applications I had written and websites I had built. Hell, even going out on my own and creating my own business, modest though it may have been, from scratch with no one to help me was an amazing achievement all by itself."

"A stupid question perhaps, but did it help?" asked Jason.

"Yes, it did. I went right back as far as the early 90's and wrote down things I had achieved and kept saying to myself, I did that. It may have been in a different lifetime, as I said, but I did it. Soon my confidence started to slowly return, and I could feel my self-esteem increasing little by little over time."

"Really?"

"Yes. You should try it some time. Then I moved to other areas of my life. The different countries I had moved to, and started from scratch in, with no friends and sometimes not even being able to speak the language, yet somehow managed to carve out a life for myself."

"Hmmm."

"Slowly, bit by bit, I felt my strength returning and I felt more in control of my life again. As time went on and I felt increasingly better, I resolved and said to myself that when Fabri contacts me again, I won't see him, because I felt sure that at some point, our paths were going to cross again."

"And did he ever contact you again?"

"Yes."

"No way!!!"

"Yeah. After he had been gone for about 8 weeks, I suddenly felt his energy again and sure enough within 3 days, he contacted me to say he was coming to Paris and wanted to meet up. The weird thing was, having blocked me and disappeared etc. He suddenly came back and contacted me exactly one year to the very day after I first arrived in Paris and felt his energy for the very first time. Coincidence?"

"You're kidding me! This is getting too weird."

"Now do you see why I stopped talking about him to people?"

"Yes, I do. However, by now you had built up your resolve, so you told him where to go, right?"

There was a bit of a pause.

"Right? repeated Jason"

"Ummm…not exactly."

"What!!!??"

"Yeah. Even though I felt I had done a lot of work and made a lot of progress, it is hard to know how far along the path you are when you don't know how long the path is, and clearly, I wasn't as far along as I thought. My resolve that I had built up and told to my friends what I would do if he ever contacted me again, instantly dissolved like a sandcastle overwhelmed by an overly boisterous wave the minute he messaged me."

"You gotta be kidding. Hadn't you learnt anything by now?"

"Well, clearly, I still had a lot to learn. However, fortunately this time the coin landed Fabri face up. He had done back-to-back flights and was exhausted. So, he didn't bring 'The Pipe Man' with him, nor was he interested in hosting anyone else. It was just us for the whole time, it was perfect and for that one night, which was probably one of the best nights of my life, I finally had everything I ever wanted."

We sat in silence for a moment while I stared wistfully into space, again, before I sighed and continued. "Eventually, of course, morning came, he left, and I went home. Then, after a few days of basking in the afterglow of that perfect night with him, I went back to continue doing the work I had started. I mean, with my resolve crumbling like that, it was clear that I still had stuff to do."

"Yeah, I guess so, but at least it all ended on a positive note, right?"

I really didn't have the strength to carry on with that right now so, to avoid responding to Jason's question and opening yet another can of worms, I glossed over it and tried to steer him away from things.

"For some reason, and I don't know what made me do it, I decided to try to step further back from everything than I had before. Suddenly, I realized the further I stepped back, the clearer I could see things. It was like standing on a mountain top where you think you can see forever, and that's when I saw it. That was the moment when all the pieces fell into place."

"What?"

I knew that if I started down that path now too, we would end up sitting there all night. So, deflecting things again, I made an excuse as I let out a tired sigh and said "Sorry Jason, it's getting late, and I am really starting to flag. I promise I will tell you about the rest in the morning."

Jason, seeing the weary look in my eyes, reluctantly agreed. We packed everything up in silence and headed off to our rooms.

Talking about Fabri like this was very emotional at times and feeling somewhat drained when I got to my master suite, I simply stripped off and collapsed into bed, looking for a good night's sleep to recharge my batteries.

CHAPTER 32

Unfortunately, sleep eluded me. Talking about Fabri so intensely, and almost reliving some of the experiences, was truly draining. Another reason why I didn't talk about him anymore.

As I lay there, almost begging for sleep to engulf me, I had the strangest sensation. A headache seemed to develop. It was like a tension headache that we all get from time to time with a feeling of pressure against the inside my head and a relentless throbbing. Yet where there was normally a centre of pain that would have me clutching my head with one hand, and diving for the paracetamols with the other, there was nothing but a vacuous void.

I had no idea what that meant and I had given up trying to fathom those things out. All I knew was each time I closed my eyes and tried to sleep, Fabri was there, filling that void with his sparkling eyes and radiant smile.

I had deflected Jason's question because the truth was Fabri had contacted me subsequently, but with various emotions boiling to the surface, and my energies strangely out of whack, I didn't feel I had the strength to go into it with Jason that evening.

Yet laying there with my eyes closed, but unable to sleep, I was once again transported back to another time and found myself remembering things I had tried so hard to bury…to forget…never wanting to face them again.

After our last magical evening together, Fabri has vanished…yet again, leaving me alone, to try to get on with things as best I can and not think about him, which is impossible. He is still on my mind every day. There is not a moment, a situation, an event or anything that does not bring my mind back to him and wishing he was here or thinking how wonderful it would be if we could have shared this or that together.

I have been trying very hard to concentrate on work and being with friends and just trying to surrender Fabri, and everything about him, to The Universe and trust that Spirit has a plan. I have continued to focus on meditation and trying to strengthen my manifestation skills, hoping I can manifest that elusive Euromillions Jackpot, so I can buy my dream house in The Caribbean and run away. I know, deep in my soul, that one day, it will happen.

However, all this and more, is just a feeble attempt to keep me from thinking about Fabri, but who am I kidding. Only those who have found the true love of their life will understand. Those fortunate enough to have that unique person remain in their lives can only imagine what the rest of us, who have not been so lucky, must endure.

Time seems to pass incredibly slowly. It's as though I can not only hear the ticking of the clock but see every individual grain of sand as it passes, in painful slow motion, though the hourglass of time. Each in its turn breaking free from the pack and having its own moment of glory as it gracefully falls, like a snowflake on a cold winter's morning, before landing delicately on the heap of those that have fallen before.

Occasionally I might get a message from Fabri out of the blue suggesting he is coming to Paris, but without feeling any energy prior to hearing from him, I am always dubious as to whether he will materialize. However, I still go through the motions of meeting him, standing outside his hotel like a faithful labrador waiting for his master's return, only to have him not appear, time and again. There's no message of cancellation, no explanation, not even a hollow apology along with some cockamamy excuse. Nothing! I am just left there, hanging, until I eventually give up and drag my weary and disappointed heart back home.

The days turn into weeks and the weeks into months and still I wait for him. Confident in my heart that somehow, someway, we will eventually be together. Unfortunately, the radio silence continues.

Then, one Saturday while I am out and about, I suddenly feel a huge surge of energy that hits me between the shoulder blades. I try to rest at a bistro, but the pain is so intense that I have no choice but to go home and go to bed, at 4 o'clock in the afternoon. It is clear in my mind that it can only be Fabri, but after all this time, I'm not sure what it means.

Unbelievably, in the early hours of the next morning, I got a text saying he is coming to Paris on the late-night flight which is due to arrive about 1:00pm Paris time. He says he will get a couple of hours' sleep first, when he arrives, and then we can meet and go for dinner. Ecstatic, I am unable to sleep for the rest of the night. My heart is doing cartwheels, and my head is bouncing with the joyous prospect of being with him once again. I knew he would come back…I just knew it!

After several hours of restlessness, I get up and do my morning routine that I had re-established, consisting of yoga, an Ab workout, followed by a smoothie and my indispensable coffee. Full of the joys of life, knowing that my baby will soon be with me again, I dive into work. Yes, it is Sunday, but the chances are I may not get much done tomorrow as he won't be departing again until lunchtime.

I diligently work all day, getting as much done as I can. He then messages me late in the afternoon and we arrange to meet in the hotel lobby, at 6:00pm. Ever punctual, eager to see him, and as excited as a dog with two tails, I arrive a few minutes early. Most of the afternoon check-ins have been completed by this time, so the lobby is quiet. Just a couple of people on laptops or mobile phones, working or possibly making plans for the evening. I take a seat off to the side and patiently wait. Bang on time, he appears from the bank of elevators. My heart, as always, skips a beat and I feel that now familiar wave of energy sweeping through me the moment I see him. Wearing jeans and a thin pink sweater that hugs every curve of his chest and arms, he flashes a slight smile and gives me a discreet nod to join him as he heads for the escalator. Naturally, I comply and am at his side in a flash. On the escalator he gives me a discreet kiss as we coolly greet each other.

We walk a short distance to find a restaurant for dinner; the time being filled with small talk and idle chitchat as we walk. Deciding on a small French bistro, we enter and find a quiet table in the corner. It is a very upmarket and modern kind of bistro. The décor has a distinctively modern Japanese influence with Imperial Jasmin Green fabrics and dark wood paneling. Unlike many bistros, the tables are well spaced, giving plenty of room for quiet conversations. Each wooden table is supported by a mixture of padded Captain's Chairs or cushioned booth seating. A brass-topped bar serves as the focal point of the main part of the bistro whilst the side areas are lined with bookshelves sporting a variety of old books. It is early and still daylight outside, though overcast, as it has been raining on and off all day. The lack of sunshine and the muted lighting of the bistro give the whole place a sort of subdued and slightly romantic atmosphere. Most people have not even thought about dinner yet, so the bistro itself is quiet, and it feels like a private dining room, just us, a waiter and a barman.

After perusing the menu, we order some food and drinks. The waiter, clearly having already had a long day, takes our order, then lazily heads for the bar with all the speed and enthusiasm of an escargot. After watching him leave, we start to talk. Ever conscious of having to curb my own enthusiasm, as I don't want him to think I am prying or interrogating him, I cautiously ask how he has been and what he has been up to with work etc. I am hoping he will come to the party and tell me why I haven't heard from him for so long, without me having to dig too much. Fortunately, he leaps straight in by apologizing that his flight schedule keeps getting changed at the last minute and, he tells me he has also been on vacation in Italy…at home with his Mum.

"Great!" I reply, "I'm glad you were able to get away for a break, you've been working so much you probably needed the rest."

"Yes" he agreed as he sits there fidgeting with the cutlery on the table and not looking at me.

"How's your Mum doing?" I ask.

"She's fine," he says.

This stilted conversation is clearly going nowhere and is obviously masking something else.

"Well, I hope you had a great time and were able to recharge your batteries," again hoping to open the conversation up a bit more.

"Yes," he agrees. Then after a pause he says, "I also needed some space to think about a few things."

Ah, ok…I think to myself. I wasn't sure what was lurking in the shadows, but here it comes! "Well, sometimes it's good to get away. A little distance can lend a certain amount of clarity and perspective to things" I waffle in a feign supportive tone, eager to keep the conversation going so that we can get to the point, that he so clearly wants to tell me, but is obviously struggling with.

"Yeah," he says unenthusiastically.

After another short pause, I ask if he managed to sort some things out.

"Yeah, I guess so," he says still not looking at me. "I stayed a week with my mum a couple of weeks ago, and we talked through a lot of things. I told her I had met someone and that it was serious. She already knows that I 'like men', so that wasn't such an issue, but I told her *we* might get married."

My heart skips about a dozen beats and I almost audibly gasp for air as I try to contain my reaction to this huge revelation. Having not discussed the topic any further since I proposed on New Year's Eve, was he really, finally, contemplating us getting married?

"What was her reaction" I ask as calmly as I possibly can, my mind racing over a million different things all at once.

"At first, she was a little upset that I was considering marrying a man. However, after we talked for some days, she finally began to accept that it is my life, and it is what I really want to do."

I reach out and place my hand on his, almost as though I am consoling him, and say "Wow. That couldn't have been an easy conversation nor a particularly comfortable time for you, but I am glad you manage to reach an understanding and maybe a level of acceptance."

"Thanks" he says. "I was a bit relieved having finally had this conversation with her and by the time I left, I felt a whole lot better about things."

"That's great, I am really pleased for you." I say as I continue to struggle to contain my excitement, and desperately want to jump right in with 'so when shall we get married' sort of thing. But before I can say anything else, he hits me with....

"So, a couple of days after I got back...*we* flew to Las Vegas and got married. We spent a week with friends in Mexico and got back yesterday, just in time for last night's flight."

Suddenly, it feels as if my whole world has imploded as what he is saying begins to sink in. My jaw drops, there is a deafening ringing in my ears, and the touch of his hand is now burning under my own.

"What?" I say, as my mind spirals and the room seems to darken until all I can see is him, still staring down at the table and fidgeting with the cutlery.

"I'm married," he murmurs as he moves his left hand towards me to show me the band of gold on his finger.

How did I not notice it before when we were walking or seated at the table. I stare at his hand and seem unable to comprehend anything. A lump begins to form in my throat that feels like the size of a bowling ball and, for a moment, I cannot even breathe. I sit there trying not to let panic wash over me and struggle to maintain some semblance of composure. After what seems like an eternity, all I can muster is "oh".

That one syllable manages to dislodge the lump in my throat. "Congratulations" I say, as I motion to the waiter that I want the bill. He looks a little perplexed as we haven't received our food yet, but he dutifully goes off to fetch it anyway.

"I hope you'll be very happy together" I say. "I hope he knows how lucky he is." Desperately trying to conceal the fact that I still don't seem to be able to breathe, I carry on. "I hope he brings you joy and happiness every day and loves you with every fiber of his being because, Fabri, you deserve nothing less."

When Fabri sees the waiter returning with the bill he asks, "What are you doing?"

"Paying the bill." I say as I now struggle to fight back the tears. "I have to go." By now my head is swirling again and a sea of emotions, one after another, are flooding over me like massive waves relentlessly pounding the rocks. The man of my dreams, the one true love of my life, the only person I have ever wanted to be married to has just gone off and married someone else.

After the waiter leaves, I start to get up from the table. Fabri grabs my hand and says "No, I don't want you to go."

As I sit back down, I feel an incredible amount of strength and courage that has suddenly surged through me while he continues to sit there with his head hanging down. "No Fabri!" I say, "What you should have said is 'I want you to stay', but you didn't…because you don't… and you never did. You've never had any real feelings for me Fabri, I have always just been a toy to you. A thing you dust off whenever you pass through Paris and then throw back on the shelf when you leave. All you ever wanted was to have someone like me to come and comfort you at night, whenever you snapped your fingers, because you are afraid to be alone."

With that I pull my hand away and stand up. For the first time since we sat down, Fabri looks up at me and I see the sadness in his eyes, but there is nothing I can do to comfort him. I feel I am on the edge of a complete emotional breakdown as my world seems to be crashing down around me. I just know I have to get away as fast as I can. With tears starting to sting my eyes, blur my vision and run down my face, I turn and stumble as quickly as possible, out of the restaurant, knocking over a chair in the process.

Fabri is left sitting there alone with tears welling up in his own eyes as he watches me clumsily flee. Moments later, outside in the street, there is a blast of a horn and the screeching of tires, followed by a dull, sickening thud. There is no need for Fabri to get up from the table or rush to the window, the screams of a woman and the ensuing commotion outside tell him all he needs to know about what has just happened.

As he sits there, now with tears starting to roll down his cheeks, perhaps he feels, maybe for the first time, my energy sweeping through him as his has always swept through me. Maybe now, he realizes, beyond any doubt, that our spiritual connection…the energies we share, which I have always been able to feel…the deep, intense love that I have for him that seems to transcend this world…the fact that I can see deep inside of him, to know who he really is, the real Fabri…it's all true.

However, worse is yet to come, because hot on the heels of this one, is the ultimate realization for him…of what he has just lost.

Suddenly aware once again of the wetness on my pillow from the emotions that had clearly been spilling out, I found myself back in the sanctuary of my master suite. As I became familiar with my surroundings again, I got up and decided I needed another shower to allow the tears to mix with the warm water and, once again, be washed down the drain forever.

CHAPTER 33

I woke up the next morning, or at least I thought it was still morning, I felt dreadful, foggy headed and really achy, as though I had been jumped in the middle of the night, wrestled to the ground and then pulled through a hedge backwards! I was also feeling a dreadful ache between my shoulder blades and, lacking any motivation to move whatsoever, I just lay there staring up at the high vaulted ceiling above the bed. I had no idea what time it was, but it must have been late. I could hear sounds of activity in the house, and the sea breeze had sprung up again.

As I slowly pulled the fragmented parts of myself back together, I wondered why I couldn't let Fabri go. I had tried everything from meditation to burning candles and sage, anything I could think of, to exorcise him from my being and consign him to the dark recesses of the past, but nothing seemed to work. I was confused and could not help but wonder as to what possible benefit there could be for him continuing to haunt me so. I guessed only time would tell. In the meantime, wherever he was, whatever he was doing and whomever he was with, I hoped he was well and that his life was full of nothing but joy and happiness. Letting out a heavy sigh, I crawled to the edge of the bed, hoisted my battered body up, stretched a little as I tried to dislodge the pain between my shoulder blades, before heading for the shower.

Having, eventually, stitched myself together as best I could, I headed out to the kitchen looking for some coffee, and lots of it.

"Good morning," I said to Mara as I entered the kitchen. She appeared to be mixing a cake or something. I really had no idea what she was doing to be honest and, frankly, at that moment, she could have been mixing gunpowder for a bomb for all I cared.

"Good morning!" She replied. "You look like hell!"

"Oh, that's a relief. I was afraid I looked like shit because that is how I feel."

"Rough night thinking about Fabri, was it?"

"Yeah."

"Are you hungry? Do you want me to make you something to eat?"

"No thanks, I don't feel like eating much right now. Maybe just a coffee and a biscuit or two."

"Well, why don't you go sit down and I'll make a fresh pot of coffee for you."

"Bless you…you are an angel," I said as I slowly made my way outside to slump on the sofa and stare at the ocean.

After a short while, Mara appeared with a pot of coffee and a pack of dark chocolate digestives. I have no idea where she got these things that are impossible to buy here, but there seemed to be no end to her resourcefulness. "Here we go, coffee as promised, and I thought these might cheer you up a bit."

"Digestives? I had no idea we had any!"

"Ah, that's because I keep them in a secret stash for just such an occasion as this."

"Thank you, Mara. I am so grateful for all you do for me."

"Well, I worry about you."

"I know you do and thank you for that too, but I will be fine once the coffee kicks in."

"Well, at least you might have a little peace for a while. Jason took himself off for a walk along the beach after breakfast. I am not sure when he will be back."

"That's probably a good thing. It will give me time to fully wake up. I am not sure I could face finishing the Fabri saga right now."

Mara just stood there looking at me for a moment, clearly wanting to say something but then thought better of it. "Ok, well, I will leave you to rest and get back to my baking."

With that Mara turned and headed back to the kitchen, while I sat there savoring the first of many cups of coffee, and almost half the packet of biscuits.

Slowly I started to recover as I worked my way through my third cup, and not a moment too soon either, as I heard the gate at the bottom of the garden open and then saw Jason emerge from the beach. He saw me and gave me a wave as he headed to the outdoor shower to wash the sand from his feet. Having then dried them, he came over to join me on the sofa.

"Hey," I said. "You want some coffee?"

"No thanks. I just had some down at the beach club, but I am sorry, I forgot to take any money with me, so I had to ask George to add it to your account. I hope you don't mind?"

"It's no problem. Don't worry about it."

"You seem a bit under the weather, are you ok?"

"Rough night, that's all."

"Really?"

"Yeah." There was a bit of a pause as Jason just sat there in silence, clearly waiting for me to continue. "I wasn't completely honest with you last night. Fabri coming back after blocking me for a couple of months, wasn't the last time I saw him, as I may have led you to believe, and memories of his subsequent and ultimate visit hounded me a bit last night."

"Oh?"

"Yeah, he came back again several months later." I then proceeded to give Jason a summary of that final visit and the fact that Fabri had gotten married.

"Wow," said Jason. "And that was it? You never heard from him again?"

"Yes, that was the last I ever heard from him. Obviously, it wasn't me that got hit by the van that night as I left the restaurant, and he could have easily discovered that, if he wanted to, however, he had his own path to follow and clearly it was without me. What can you do?" I shrugged.

"Not a lot, I guess."

There was a brief pause as Jason sat there thinking about things before continuing. "So, last night, before we went to bed, you were saying something about stepping back and seeing things more clearly, like you had some sort of epiphany or something. What was that all about?"

"Yeah, that was when all the pieces fell into place, and I realized what he was and what he had been doing."

"You mean that was when you realized he was…what did you call him…your teacher, and the missing piece of your soul?"

"Yes"

"So, what was he doing exactly?"

CHAPTER 34

"I think I may have already said this to you before, but when I left Porto, I was a complete mess, though I didn't know it at the time. When I looked back over my life from a much higher perspective, I was in such a bad state that I didn't even recognize myself anymore."

"Really? How do you mean?" asked Jason.

"I no longer resembled the person I thought I was. It was clear that I had been trying to fill a void in my life left behind after the relationship with Anna ended. I realized, at that time, that maybe for the previous 10 years or so, I had been compromising myself in various ways, maybe because I was desperate to have someone in my life. I had been doing things against my nature or even just things I don't like such as tolerating Fabri's games, just to have someone…to give my life some meaning again."

"Wow, that must have been quite a revelation?"

"Yeah, for sure. So, for years, I ran round from person to person, both men and women, trying to be the person that I thought each of them wanted, instead of being myself, just to find some way to fill the massive hole in my life. However, obviously, every time it went wrong, I was left rejected, sometimes in a very cruel way, and that person would then vanish, never to be seen again. I was always left behind thinking I did everything I could to make it work when, really, I was simply opening myself up, each time, to being used and abused, which almost always happened. Each rejection tarnished my self-esteem and left a layer of doubt over my own self-worth. Eventually I started to believe that I was not enough for these people and that there must be something wrong with me, which clearly there was."

"Ok, but I don't get why you didn't recognize yourself, I mean you were still you, right?"

"Deep down yes, I believed I was still me, but that was not how I appeared to everyone else."

"Hmmm…" mused Jason.

"Ok, imagine this. Have you ever gone to a wharf down by the harbor and seen those mooring bollards that they use to moor ships to the wharf?"

"Yeah?"

"And sometimes those mooring bollards are fixed to the wharf by giant nuts screwed onto large bolts that stick up from the surface of the wharf, right?"

"Yeah, I guess so?"

"So, because the harbor is a salty environment, over time the salts build up on these nuts, calcifying layer upon layer until they no longer look like the original nut. Sure, the nut is still there underneath, doing its job, however, on the surface it now just looks like a large, calcified, salty blob. And, metaphorically speaking, that is basically what I was."

"Seriously?"

"Yes. Like the salt calcification at the wharf, each rejection added more tarnish on my self-esteem and cast another layer of doubt on my self-worth, until they changed how I appeared and presented myself to the world. Negative, moaning and always expressing inadequacy in my relationships with others. Not to mention lethargy and general apathy in other areas of my life such as work, health etc. It was effectively a downward spiral over many years."

"Wow."

"What Fabri had been doing, whether he was conscious of the fact or not, and I suspect not, was breaking down the layers of calcified self-doubt. From my elevated perspective I saw the pattern that had been happening. He would break me down with his actions or words and then leave me to reflect on things, on my own, by ignoring and ghosting me. Then he would come back to check on me and see how I was doing. At that point, if he felt he needed to, he would hit me again, breaking away more layers, consequently raising my self-esteem and rebuilding my self-worth as I fought back, until eventually, I reached the point where I am at now. Remembering my old self, the person I once was and the things I had achieved in my life. Finally resembling who I really was underneath and being able to present that person to the world once again."

"You're kidding me?!"

"No, I am not. Each time he would give me a harder thing to work on which would require more time. That's why the gap between his visits almost doubled every time from 1 week, to 2 weeks, to 1 month, to 2 months, to 4 months. During those times I began finding more power and energy within myself instead of constantly looking for an energy source within others, like the energy I felt when I first came to Paris, and all of this was led by Fabri."

"Forgive me for saying this," said Jason, "but are you sure this wasn't just your overactive imagination at work?"

"It's ok. I know how it sounds, and many people have asked the same question but no, I am sure this wasn't just my imagination or wishful thinking or some sort of idolizing of Fabri and hero worship. I have always said that I saw two layers when I looked at Fabri. An outer layer that he shows to the world, which to me has always been transparent, and an inner layer which is what I believe to be the real him. It is this inner layer that holds his heart that radiates light and energy like a galaxy of a million stars and was the source for all that he did. I believe the real Fabri, this inner layer, is a highly evolved spirit, possibly a spirit-guide working through the outer layer, to whom I am somehow spiritually connected. Almost as though he is part of my very soul. Who drew me into its circle to help me remember who I once was. To help me regain my own strength and self-worth and stand on my own two feet again without compromising myself to please other people."

There was a long pause as I let Jason absorb what I was saying.

"That's unbelievable!" said Jason finally.

"Yeah, now do you understand why I am reluctant to talk about him?"

"Yes, because it just sounds ridiculously crazy. However, if you are spiritually connected to him and he is a part of your soul, as you say, is that why you've never been able to let him go, even after he ran off and married someone else?"

"Yeah, I think so."

"Didn't you ever try to move on and meet someone else?"

"Oh yeah, and that was a bit bizarre as well," I chuckled.

CHAPTER 35

"Oh no! I think I am afraid to ask", sighed Jason. "What happened?"

"I tried listening to my friends who kept telling me to move on and find someone else, but I found it very hard to begin with."

"Really, why?"

"I was so in love with Fabri he really had become part of my soul, and I am a very loyal person. For about a year after I met him, even after I knew I had seen him for the last time, I couldn't even look at another guy."

"Really?!"

"Yeah, really. I could pass the most amazing looking guy in the street, checking me out, and I'd think 'wow, he's gorgeous!', but then my next immediate thought was, 'but he's not Fabri and all I want is my baby', and I'd keep on walking."

"Seriously? You eventually got over that though, right?"

"I had to. I was in danger of becoming a recluse. I forced myself to get back on the apps and go out 'cruising' bars again. It was a little uncomfortable at first and I even felt a little guilty, like I was doing something wrong behind his back, but eventually I started to meet guys again. Nothing really gelled though. Still, everything happens for a reason, and I learnt a few things from that too."

"Like what?"

"Like Spirit has a plan and no matter how hard you try, you simply can't make things happen that aren't in alignment with that plan."

"Really?"

"Yep, I dated lots of different types of guys thinking perhaps the problem was I was chasing the wrong type, but it didn't matter what they were like or what age they were or anything. Things always ended up the same way. I even made the mistake of going on a date with a guy because he reminded me of Fabri and I thought he might be the ideal replacement to knock Fabri off his pedestal."

"What happened?"

"I knew this Spanish guy, Miguel, sort of from a distance, through a social group. I always fancied him since the first time I saw him, but I never got the 'oh, maybe he fancies me' vibe, so I never pursued anything. However, after a couple of months of hanging out with friends in the hope that fate would intervene and the man of my dreams would somehow cross my path, I discovered an online message from Miguel thanking me for having a beer with him the previous week at a function we both attended. Naturally, I responded which suddenly opened the flood gates and he started messaging me like crazy. This was totally out of the blue and unexpected, and I have to say very exciting because I did fancy him. Within an hour or so we had firmed up a first date."

"Just like that…again?"

"Yep. As you are possibly starting to see, when things are in alignment with Spirit's plan, they happen, just like that."

"Yeah, so it seems."

"Anyway, the following Friday, we met at the Rodin Museum near Hotel des Invalides in Paris. Being super excited and not wanting to risk being late, I overcompensated and arrived about 30 minutes beforehand. It was a gorgeous, late summer afternoon with the sun shining and a gentle breeze wafting through the trees, so I decided to sit for a while in the Square d'Ajaccio next to the Hotel des Invalides. It was wonderful to be sitting in a quiet park in Paris, watching couples spending time together as they sat on various benches, surrounded by manicured lawns and flowerbeds in full bloom, with the Eiffel Tower as a backdrop. Even though I was alone, I couldn't help but start to feel the romantic vibe that so obviously filled the air.

After a short while, I decided it was time to head to the Museum and, as I approached the entrance, I found Miguel already waiting for me, relaxing as he propped himself up on one of the security bollards out front. With his earbuds in his ears and absorbed in whatever he was looking at on his mobile phone, he was completely oblivious to my arrival. I watched him intently as I approached, and he was just as gorgeous as I remembered. He was 6 feet tall and dressed all in black, which matched his jet-black hair, and offset his deep, dark chocolate, brown eyes and the clean shaven, flawless olive skin of his face. I couldn't help but feel unbelievably privileged to be meeting him and was silently thanking the fates for their intervention."

"Oh no…here we go again!" said Jason as he facepalmed his forehead.

Choosing to ignore his remark, I continued. "After a brief hello with a kiss on each cheek in typical French fashion, we went inside. The Museum was bigger than I expected and was truly amazing. Miguel's knowledge of Art History and Sculpture was an incredible bonus for me as it was like having my own personal tour guide. We wandered around the sculptures, sometimes together, sometimes moving at our own pace only to meet up again at the next piece. All the while I was becoming more attracted to this gorgeous, sexy man. Sometimes, I would catch myself, discretely, studying his form and the way his shirt stretched across his chest and how his jeans hugged his butt and clung to his thighs. Occasionally, we would study the same piece, and he would stand right behind me, but without touching me. However, he was so close that I could feel his energy and warmth that naturally radiated from him along with the intoxicating heavenly aroma of his cologne. Every time, I desperately wanted him to reach out and break the touch barrier, but he didn't. By the time we got halfway through the exhibition, the flames of my romantic mood, which started in the park, were now being fanned like a forest fire by his presence, and some of the incredibly moving sculptures like Rodin's 'The Kiss'. My emotions now seemed to be bubbling out of control inside me. I found myself even getting aroused and desperately wanted to kiss him, but still, he didn't make a move. He was the perfect gentleman and even though he was tantalizingly close I also, somehow, managed to restrain myself from making a move for fear of embarrassing myself if this was all just in my head."

"So, what happened?"

"After a stroll in the beautiful gardens, and both being completely satiated with the works of Rodin, we decided to return to a bistro, close to my apartment, where we shared a bottle of wine, and we talked and talked and talked some more. The conversation flowed effortlessly between us. I found him fascinating to listen to as he seemed to be extremely well read, and you know how much of a sapiophile I am! I also found him to be a great listener too as I probably talked his ear off about what must have seemed like the most mundane things in the world. I quickly found my feelings deepening as the afternoon turned into evening, and as neither of us seemed keen for the date to end, we went for dinner, lots more talking, and a short walk before ending back to my place for yet another bottle of wine."

"Ah, now we are getting somewhere!" Said Jason with a gleeful smile on his face.

"It was there, on the terrace, that he finally made a move and damn, was it ever worth the excruciating wait. In mid-conversation, he simply stood-up, stooped over me as he took my face in his hands and kissed me, just like Fabri did…and Francisco before him. It was intense, yet gentle, full of fire and passion, yet sweet and sensual, all at the same time. That was it for me. I was a goner, again, and desperately wanted this gorgeous, real-life sculpture before me. However, I hopelessly tried to play it cool, pushed him back a little and told him, if he was going to kiss me like that, I would be wanting to see him again."

"What did he say?"

"He flashed a smile at me that was as bright as the moon above us and confirmed that he was more than fine with that. With such validation, echoing in my ears along with the thunderous beat of my own, exploding heart, we quickly moved inside and, obviously, into bed. A couple of hours of passion passed in the blink of an eye and before long he needed to get the last train home. Slightly disappointed that he couldn't stay the night, oh how I wanted to sleep wrapped in his muscular arms with my legs intertwined with his, I reluctantly let him go."

"This is starting to sound all too familiar," mused Jason

"Yeah, unable to get he him out of my head, I spent the next couple of days in a now all too familiar daydream. Not wanting to seem too eager or clingy, I waited a respectable amount of time, before finding a convenient reason to reach out to him. We had a brief exchange of messages but then, in mid conversation, like a disappearing mirage of an oasis in the desert, he vanished, just like that, and I never heard from again."

"You're kidding?!"

"Nope. I never thought for one minute that someone could be so engaging, encouraging and totally immersed in a date with someone and yet, in fact, be nothing more than a master game player the whole time."

"Ouch! That must have hurt?"

"Actually, not as much as you might think. I was super attracted to him because in so many ways, he reminded me of Fabri, even to the point that I started experiencing all the same emotions I had every time Fabri ghosted or blocked me, but that is when it dawned on me…"

"What?"

"He was just an echo of the person I really wanted and, like all echoes, he had no substance. With that realization I quickly moved on and never looked back."

CHAPTER 36

"Afternoon teatime" announced Mara as she emerged from the kitchen with the cake she had been baking, still warm from the oven, a few sandwiches and a large pot of tea as Paulo, whose timing was always impeccable, suddenly appeared from nowhere to join us.

"I still don't get it," said Jason. "I mean, I know I probably haven't had nearly as much experience as you, but I have had guys treat me bad too. However, the minute they do I just block them and move on. So, even though you felt spiritually connected to Fabri, I still struggle to understand why you didn't do the same thing? Why you kept going back to him, allowing that connection to develop more deeply, even though you told friends you wouldn't see him again."

"I am still not sure I fully know the answer to that myself. However, when I looked back on my entire life I saw something that may be part of the reason, and it has to do with energy."

"Huh?" said Jason

"Let me see if I can explain. Now I don't know if this is normal or the same for everyone, but I came to realize that I have been looking for something my entire life. Something that has always been missing that I needed to make me whole as an entity, to complete my soul, as it were."

Jason just sat there staring at me and said nothing, so I continued.

"Having done some reading, some experts say it may be the result of a childhood trauma, that something is stolen from us when we are young, and we spend our whole life trying to get it back. However, I feel I came *into* this current reality with that piece already missing and I have been on a mission ever since to find it. Maybe it was something stolen from me during a past life. Or maybe it is some elaborate game created by the Universe to give me a purpose, a reason to have the experiences from which to learn and spiritually evolve. I don't know, but I certainly believe I did learn and evolve after spending all that time with Fabri. That is something I may well have missed out on, had I simply walked away at the beginning."

"Ok, so I get it that you gained a lot by staying with him, but was it worth all the pain etc.?"

"Yes, it is only now with hindsight that I can pinpoint significant times, events and people in my life, that were clearly clues given to me along the way, to help me identify what I was supposed to be looking for"

"Which was…? asked Jason.

"Strong masculine energy."

"Wait, so are you saying you went through all of that just because he is masculine and you like masculine men?"

"Well, kind of. You know how when two magnets get close enough, they just snap together?"

"Yeah," said Jason, again unsure where I was going with this.

"Well, when Fabri started to get closer to me, the times when he did come to Paris, I would feel his energy as I said. Then when he got close enough, we would just snap together like two magnets."

"Seriously?!! said Jason. "And you think this sort of thing has been happening your whole life?"

"Yes, since day one. Let me give you an example. Not long after I was born, my parents separated and there was a time, I have been told, back before my earliest memories, when I would cry, unconsolably. There was nothing my mother could do to pacify me, I simply cried, bawled and probably screamed, seemingly without reason. That is, until in sheer frustration, she handed me to my uncle, and the moment I was placed in his arms, I immediately stopped crying. At the time I am sure it must have seemed odd, maybe even perplexing to everyone, but with retrospect, the answer is clear to me now. It was because of my uncle's masculine energy. Perhaps it was the first time I was aware of the missing piece, and maybe the first time I thought I had found it, and it happened before I could even talk."

"Seriously?" said Jason.

"Yes, and there have been other numerous times where I now notice similar things have happened. Looking back, it is also no surprise to me now, that almost all the people that have had a significant impact on my life, have all been male."

Everyone just sat in silence staring at me as I continued.

"With that revelation, it is no wonder that I fell so heavily in love with Francisco who had that same masculine energy. It is also no surprise that I cried, unconsolably, when he ended things and suddenly took that source of masculine energy away from me. I was immediately catapulted back to that crying infant. Only now I didn't have the luxury of an obliging male figure to console me. So undeterred, I embarked on seeking through Grindr, and various other avenues, that missing piece of my soul which I desperately needed to find, but without success. That is, until I was drawn to Paris and met Fabri."

"Wow, that's incredible," said Jason as he began to understand what it was that I was explaining to him.

"I don't know if it is age, experience, the time spent on self-development or just being an overthinker that hones us in on what it is we are looking for. However, as age begins to play a part, the places where I can find what I am looking for become fewer and farther between, and the harder the search for that masculine energy becomes. Perhaps that also partly explains why I kept going back to where I knew it existed, in Fabri, instead of just throwing him away at the beginning. However, whilst my search may have less opportunities these days, like searching for the Holy Grail, it is a lifelong quest that will never end until I find it."

Jason was lost for words at this point and just sat there staring at me.

"It reminds me of a snippet of a poem that has probably been overused in books, television and films to the extent that it is possibly now a cliché, but it is the words of Tennyson that most succinctly sums up my aged perspective:

> We are not now that strength which in old days Moved earth and heaven, that which we are, we are, One equal temper of heroic hearts, Made weak by time and fate, but strong in will To strive, to seek, to find, and not to yield.

CHAPTER 37

"Ok, so what happens now? You retreated here to what, live alone? I mean this place isn't particularly gay friendly nor teaming with gay men. So, what are you going to do…sit here alone until you die?" asked Jason.

"I don't know, but I am now certain that Spirit has a plan." I said as I shrugged my shoulders. "It's been more than 5 years since that evening in the bistro when I last saw Fabri and whatever transpired that night, there is no getting away from the fact that his path was different to mine which led him into marrying someone else. I have no idea if that made him happy, but I hope so. Maybe it was all part of some plan to teach me the things I have learned and to strengthen my beliefs."

"Ok, so what is it you believe?" asked Jason.

"Well, I now believe we are predominately all connected to an energy source. That we are a spiritual being having a temporary human experience as many books, by people like Dr Wayne W. Dyer, will tell you. I think our energies vibrate at varying frequencies, and we connect with each other according to the frequency of our vibrations. I think it is how we choose our friends and partners because, subconsciously, we feel their vibrational frequency, and the closer they vibrate to our own, the more they mean to us."

"Really?"

"Sure. Ask yourself, have you ever met someone you instantly didn't like? Ever said to someone that so and so gives me the willies or the 'heebie-jeebies'?

"Yeah, of course, but no one says willies or heebie-jeebies anymore uncle!"

I cocked my head at him but chose to ignore the jibe and said, "Well, maybe it's because the frequency they vibrated at was too different from your own."

"Hmmm, maybe," conceded Jason.

"Then, of course, there is the other extreme, when we meet someone who is on the same frequency as us. The minute we feel it we have an instant attraction to that person. Maybe, to understand and rationalise this, we pass it off as love at first sight. That's how it was for me with Fabri. We were on the same frequency, and I believe that his vibration was so strong, and so close to my own, that I could feel him whenever our paths began to converge.

"Ok, I get that you were madly in love with him but, surely by now you can just let him go and find someone else?"

"The short answer is no. Plenty of people told me to 'forget about him', 'move on', 'you'll meet someone else', 'you deserve better than him', and lots of other variations on the same theme, but the truth is, you never get over something that is part of you, part of your soul, as Fabri was to me. You just learn to live with it…or without it in this case."

"But he didn't want to be with you. Clearly, he didn't love you, so why do you hang on to these feelings? Aren't you just torturing yourself? Let it go!"

"I'm not so sure about that. Maybe I am wrong, but he is the only person who kept coming back after repeatedly breaking up with me. I don't think he would have done that if he didn't feel something too."

"So, are you saying you'll never get over him…ever? That's it… end of story?!"

"Maybe, I don't know. Don't misunderstand me. Though I think about him most days, I am not moping around wishing for something that is not going to happen. I am getting on with my life and doing my work and following my path wherever it takes me and keeping my eyes open for anyone that might cross my path. However, even after all this time, my feelings for him are just as strong as ever."

"I see…I think," said Jason with an unconvinced look on his face.

"That was another thing I have learned over the years. That love exists on many different levels and to different degrees. My relationship with Anna lasted 15 years and was wonderful and I would never exchange those years for anything. Then there was Francisco who to me, at the time, was the ultimate and I never believed anyone would knock him off his pedestal, that is until I met Fabri. None of these were any better or worse than the other but what I felt with Fabri, was different. That is why, despite everything else, he was and always will be, the one true love of my life to whom I owe so much, which is why I believe him to be the missing piece of my soul."

"Ok, I think I get it, and I am grateful for you sharing all of this with me, but I don't see how this helps me to tell one guy from the next. Whom I should stick with and whom I should throw away because every time I meet someone, I think they are the one. Are you telling me I have to go through something like what you did, just to be able to step back and tell the difference?" asked Jason.

"Well, sometimes in this life, you gotta kiss a lot of frogs before you find your prince," I chortled.

"Thanks, yeah, that's really helpful!" retorted Jason.

"Ok, sorry. Maybe you do need to step back and look objectively at why you are attracted to these people, consult your list of what it is you want from a guy, and try to work out what it is they want from you. Is it just a superficial lust, purely physical attraction, or something deeper?"

"How can I tell? I don't think I can just ask outright what they want. They'll think I am crazy".

"Well, try keeping a diary, I know it sounds geeky, but you'll be amazed how quickly patterns reveal themselves."

"A diary??!! Are you serious? Who do I look like? Bridget Jones??!!"

"Very funny, but yes, I am serious" I said. "Constantly look at how things go, write down how people treat you and how they react to things. Before long they will reveal their true nature and then you will know what it is they truly want from you. Review what you write on a regular basis and before you know it, you'll be able to spot the user, the narcissist, the manipulator and the game player from a mile away."

"Really?"

"Yes, really. Give it a go. You may also learn a thing or two about yourself which is never a bad thing."

"Hmmm…that sounds pretty anal if you ask me."

"Well, that may be true. For many years I had a friend who used to tell me the same thing, to keep a diary, and like you, I always poo pooed the idea. It was only once I was trying to make sense of things with Fabri that I began to do it, and once I started, it opened a whole world of ah-ha moments for me and gave me more clarity over things than I could ever have imagined possible."

"Really?"

"Yes, it was the only way that I was able to get my head straight, look at things clearly and learn the things I did."

"You make it all sound so simple."

"If only it were. The modern world makes it much more complicated and probably stops us listening to the vibrations of others. We seem to have forgotten that happiness depends on harmony. Instead, we live in a disposable world and that now seems to apply to relationships too. We have apps for this and that and everything seems to hang on whether we swipe left or right."

"I know," sighed Jason. "The apps are horrible, but everyone is on them, and it seems to be the only way to meet people these days. What else am I supposed to do?"

"Well, based on personal experience, I would suggest you ditch the apps, don't play the modern game but instead, work on yourself, trust that Spirit has a plan and let whoever you are meant to be with, find you."

"Work on myself by doing what? I already go to the gym 3 times a week."

"That's great but I was thinking more of things like meditation, raising your vibrational energies and never underestimate the power of handwriting a gratitude journal every day, which is different from keeping a diary. I know it all sounds very hippy, but it really makes a difference. Also, think critically about everything. The News, what you read about on social media, influencers, celebrity magazines, sales pitches for this and that, the actions of those close to you and even your own behaviour on a day-to-day basis. Paying attention to these things and even limiting your consumption of some of them, will help you to monitor your own vibrational frequency, and will also help you to avoid things, people and situations that might lower it. That will give you a clearer insight into yourself and the world around you."

"I don't know," sighed Jason. "It all sounds like such a lot of hard work."

Somewhere off in the distance, there was a ding-dong from the front gate. "Oh, that's probably the laundry people," said Mara as she got to her feet and headed off to deal with things.

"This is all getting too heavy for me," said Paulo. "I think I'll go and help Mara," and with that he got up and followed her.

After watching them go, I turned back to Jason, "Well, it's up to you, but these are all the things that I learnt from Fabri, and he changed my life like no one else ever has. However, if you don't want to do all those things, there is an alternative."

"Which is?", asked Jason.

"You could simple just surrender everything to a higher power, and trust that Spirit has a plan for you, as I believe it does for all of us."

"Hmmm" mused Jason.

"What does that mean? That you'll try to do some of these things?"

There was a long pause, and I just sat there looking at Jason, waiting for him to make up his mind.

"Okay, okay, I'll try uncle. I promise."

"Good. Now you'll have to excuse me for a minute. Too much coffee and nature calls!"

As I got up from the sofa and started to head towards the guest bathroom, Jason sighed and said, "I wish life wasn't so complicated."

"Actually, I don't think life is complicated. I think we just make it so."

Just then Mara came out from the kitchen with a concerned look on her face.

"Ummm...sorry to interrupt, but there's someone here to see you."

"Oh?" I said, "I thought I was picking Mel up from the airport tomorrow?"

"It's not Mel...He says his name is Fabri," said Mara, her voice trembling.

"What!!" exclaimed Jason, "You can't be serious??!!"

I stared at Mara for a moment, a little dumbfounded but strangely enough, not that surprised as I recalled the pain between my shoulder blades that I had been feeling and put two and two together. "Oh no!" was all I could say.

"He's in the kitchen with Paulo. Look, we can just tell him that you are not available, and Paulo can get rid of him. Please?!" begged Mara.

"No, it's ok." I said after a moment. "I'll be there in a moment."

"You're not actually going to see him, are you?!" exclaimed Jason

"Yes, I am going to go and see him."

"But he was horrible to you!"

"Yeah"

"He played with you, lied to you and manipulated you!"

"Yes"

"He went off and married someone else!"

"You don't need to remind me!"

"So why the hell are you going to see him!? Just get Paulo to send him away."

"To find out why he is here. Maybe, because despite everything, I know who he really is deep inside and maybe because he has always been, and always will be, the one true love of my life…"

"Seriously??!!" said Jason somewhat exasperated.

"…and maybe because the last time I saw that missing piece of my soul, that I so desperately seek, it was in his arms."

With that, I turned and headed towards the kitchen.

ABOUT THE AUTHOR

Having spent my life switching between heterosexual and now gay relationships, I find myself living in a much larger gay community. I have been continuing my spiritual awakening journey and deepening my own personal understanding of people, relationships and the world around us. I have done a substantial amount of reading and recently become almost a disciple of Dr Wayne W. Dyer, having read so many of his books and trying to live by his teachings.

By day I am a digital nomad, one of the originals having worked this way for almost 30 years. However, I am spending more time doing creative writing these days as I find it an excellent outlet for my overactive imagination. As I slowly advance in years, I am also finding I am becoming more of a source of wisdom for the younger people around me, as I work to combine my life experiences with the things I have learnt. I am certainly no expert, but I feel I am developing a greater understanding for myself of this life we live, and I want to pass what I have learnt, more easily, onto others through my writing.

www.ingramcontent.com/pod-product-compliance
Ingram Content Group UK Ltd.
Pitfield, Milton Keynes, MK11 3LW, UK
UKHW042029130226
467991UK00004B/32